STRANGE ENCHANTMENT

Ariadne was pleased when her father was invited to go back to Xanos to excavate a temple. It had been ten years since their last visit to the Greek island, which had been her mother's home ... But it was not the homecoming Ariadne expected. There was mystery about her mother's death, and about the strange Paulo Gavalas — who owned more than half the island — and his cousin Michael. What connection did the handsome Paulo have with her own and her mother's past?

IRENE ORD

---◆---

STRANGE ENCHANTMENT

511131

Complete and Unabridged

LINFORD
Leicester

First published in Great Britain in 1979 by
Robert Hale Limited
London

First Linford Edition
published 1999
by arrangement with
Robert Hale Limited
London

British Library CIP Data

Ord, Irene
   Strange enchantment.—Large print ed.—
Linford romance library
1. Love stories
2. Large type books
I. Title
823.9'14 [F]

ISBN 0–7089–5488–X

Published by
F. A. Thorpe (Publishing) Ltd.
Anstey, Leicestershire

Set by Words & Graphics Ltd.
Anstey, Leicestershire
Printed and bound in Great Britain by
T. J. International Ltd., Padstow, Cornwall

This book is printed on acid-free paper

1

Ariadne watched the blurred lines of the island become larger and clearer. Xanos! The Greek island where she had spent so many happy years as a child, and where her whole life had changed after the tragic death of her mother.

She watched the sun change the hazy lines of grey to sharper hues of blue and green and purple. The small white boxes meandering up the cliff-side turned into flat-roofed houses. The ferry-boat from Athens was crowded with holiday-makers, islanders back from a visit to the mainland, and merchandise. She glanced up at her father standing motionless and stern, his face not revealing his thoughts.

She tucked an arm into his.

'Glad to be back, Dad? How long is it now?'

'Ten years, and . . . yes, four months. It's a long time, an eternity.'

'Perhaps we shouldn't have come. Someone else could have done the excavation. The island will surely have changed.'

But she was wrong. The ferry chugged into the little harbour and swung into an arc to come up against the wharf which she recognised immediately. Still the same old pilings, a little more patched, and the same smell of fish and rotting smell of seaweed. Huge blocks of white and cream marble, finely veined, stood waiting to be shipped as in the past. Xanos, along with several of the other islands still exported a certain amount of marble.

The Greek harbour-master, fussy as ever, was there to welcome the passengers from the ship. Takis Pappadopolous was a little fatter, and his black curly hair more grizzled but the smile was the same.

'Professor! Welcome once again to

2

Xanos! It has been too long. And you Miss Ariadne. Poss íste? How are you?'

'Póli kalá efháristo. Very well, thanks.' The answer in Greek had been automatic, but rusty. It had been a long time since she chattered in Greek. She smiled at Takis, and suddenly he was kissing her in welcome, and tears came into his eyes.

'We missed you here on Xanos. It is good you both are back.'

'I am afraid we are not back for good, Takis. I am working for the Greek Government again, and will be in charge of the excavations that were started fifteen years ago. I shall be here for as long as it takes to finish the project, and after that . . . who knows?'

'Well, we must make the most of your visit, and try and persuade you to stay. There is a reservation for you at the Mykonos Hotel. A message came from the Director of the Ministry of Excavation. All the members of the

3

project are to stay at the Mykonos.'

'Thank you, Takis. And how is Katerina, and your son?'

'Very well. Katerina looks forward to meeting you again. She is a little plumper,' he grinned, 'a good cook, is Katerina. And Miklos has grown to manhood and eats like a mountain goat!' Takis was very proud of his only son. He was blessed with four daughters, but of these he said nothing.

'And what of those pretty daughters of yours?' Takis shrugged.

'Two are married and both have children, and Annalika is to be married soon, and young Katya is away on the mainland. She wants to be a teacher!' He spat in the dust in disgust. 'Her mother spoils her. She should be at home helping in the house, but no! Her mother says if the girl wants to better herself, who are we to stop her. Then she complains about having no help! Bah! Women!'

'So you only have Annalika and Miklos at home. Very different to the old days when your house was overflowing and full of noise and laughter.'

'Well, that was ten years ago. We are all a little older. And Ariadne here, grown up, and as beautiful as we expected her to be. It is good to have old friends back.' He cleared his throat, and shouted after a lingering figure in the background.

'Petros! Get that luggage sorted out and see it all gets to the Mykonos Hotel. And mind none of it gets left behind . . . And be careful of those boxes over there . . . Specimen cases, I take it?'

Professor Powis nodded.

'They are well packed for the journey. Are some of the other members of the team here yet? I understand Stephanos Papitsis was to come a few days earlier.'

'Oh yes, O-kirios Papitsis is here and already arranging the camp. Several other young men accompanied him, and a very solemn young lady in

5

heavy black glasses. Frightening, she was. So efficient, more like a man.' He shuddered. 'Heaven preserve me from such a one!' The Professor laughed.

'Poor Miss Fafoutis! If she heard you she would be hurt. A good woman to work with, and has a good command of English. Her only fault is that she is shortsighted, hence the formidable glasses!'

'Do I know her, Dad? I seem to remember the name. She wasn't the little dark girl who recorded all your finds? I remember . . . '

'Yes, Eugenie. You used to tease the life out of her. She must be all of thirty or more now. I wonder if she has changed . . . The Director wrote and told me she was still working for them and would be coming on this little venture. Come, Ariadne, let us make our way to the Mykonos. I want a bath and a change, and a glass of ouzo before dinner.'

Their rooms were comfortable, but the plumbing a little primitive which

6

was no surprise to either of them. White-washed walls, and each room with an icon over the bed, which was covered with a highly coloured hand-woven blanket. The floors were tiled in small mosaic patterns and here and there a native rug was laid. The effect was of space and coolness. The windows had shutters, and Ariadne remembered that the meltemi winds could blow without warning. The windows could be closed and barred in a matter of minutes, keeping out grit-laden dust until the fierce wind died down as quickly as it came.

A huge cupboard built into an alcove took all her clothes. She hung up all that could suffer in transit. It made the room appear more like home. Her brushes with her mother's initials on them in chased silver were placed on the dressing chest and then it seemed as if she had never been away from Xanos. It was just such another room that had been hers so many years ago. But now there was no laughing mother . . . the beautiful Nina Kavouras, married to the English Professor . . . Ariadne sighed and took out her mother's photograph in the silver frame. She was very like Ariadne with her hair blowing in the wind. She was smiling and waving, and behind her loomed the rocks from where she had plunged to her death so tragically later on . . . Ariadne placed it on the chest, where she could see it when she was in bed. Somehow, coming back had brought it all to the forefront of her mind again. How much worse would it be for her father?

Downstairs, Ariadne found her father talking to Stephanos Papitsis, a stocky man with rather bowed legs and a curly black beard. He extended a broad hand in a firm greeting. He looked to be a man of thirty-five or more, and made her uncomfortable by his boldly appraising look. She turned abruptly away, and encountered Miss Fafoutis' eye. She smiled and beckoned her over to her table.

'Ah, the little Ariadne! The little

tease. How are you? You have grown very like your mother . . . ' She stopped, and a look which Ariadne could not define, was gone before it was there. A look of distaste? No, it could not have been that! Ariadne was puzzled.

'Yes, I am supposed to be like Mother. You are Miss Fafoutis? Is anything the matter? You look . . . '

'Nothing is the matter.' She smiled however, with an effort. 'And please do not be so formal. You used to call me Eugenie . . . ' Then her face was transformed by a genuine smile. 'Do you remember chasing me along that stony beach with that very dead octopus you had got from that fisherboy? And how its tentacles waved and snaked about, and I threatened to tell your Father?'

'And you never did, and we became great friends after that.'

They smiled at each other. The years fell away and it was as if they had always been friends. Eugenie took off the formidable black-framed glasses to polish them and Ariadne saw the warm velvety-black eyes they hid, and wondered how it was possible that Takis Pappadopolous could think she was frightening.

Eugenie introduced her to the other members of the team. Stavros and Petros, students from the College in Athens. Both brawny carefree boys willing to dig and learn . . . and the thin Elias Haralambos with the pointed face of an elf, whose only interest in life was tracing the Minoan Dynasty. His conversation consisted of a series of miniature lectures, and unless one was sufficiently interested, he was just a plain bore.

There was another man yet to come. Eugenie explained about him. She had already met him in Athens. Alexander Zarras. A gentle giant of a man who was an expert on treasure trove. He had been called in several times by the Government to find gold, a cache of hidden relics or perhaps the proceeds of robberies. He had a knack for smelling out ancient burial-grounds, and now his task was to help Stephanos Papitsis in finding a hidden hoard of Nazi gold.

Ariadne opened her eyes wide. Eugenie smiled at Ariadne's astonishment.

'Did you never hear any stories of the cache? A U-boat reputedly carrying gold for Hitler's getaway was blown off course and was making for Crete. She was sighted by the allies when she surfaced and then there was a long game of hide-and-seek. Then for a long time there was no clue as to her whereabouts. She reappeared somewhere between Xanos and Siros and was finally despatched off the coast of the Island of Tinos. Several men were saved, but not the Captain, and one man talked about the bullion they were carrying.'

'Did it not go down in the submarine?'

'According to the man it was taken ashore, but he was not one of the crew detailed to unload it. All he knew was that it was taken ashore on a small island.'

11

'But there are hundreds of small islands in the Cyclades! What makes the Government think it could be Xanos?'

'They don't. It is a matter of elimination, and the log-book. The U-boat was raised a few years ago, and the ship's log was found. There was evidence that a bulky consignment of sorts had been carried, and unloaded, and Siros has already been examined with a fine tooth-comb, so now Xanos is to be considered.'

'It is all very exciting. Just fancy, we might be sitting on a fortune!'

'It could be. Some of the older villagers remember the Germans coming ashore for water and vegetables, and the U-boat remaining on the surface for two nights, diving during the day and then she was gone. Most people were frightened and kept indoors, and so knew nothing of what happened.'

'And this Mr. Zarras might be able to ferret out the hiding-place?'

'He knows how the Nazi mind

12

worked. If anyone can find it, he will.'

'I shall look forward to meeting him.'

Several days went by. Now Ariadne had found her bearings and visited the places she remembered from childhood. The rocky shingle where she and the village children played. The vineyard that straggled outside the little town where old George Catacousinos grew and pressed his grapes making the rough local wine. Now, it was a younger George Catacousinos with a fresh-faced wife and two small children scuffling about in the dusty yard.

She and her father walked out into the hills and visited old picnic spots. She watched the shadows form on her father's face and so she did not encourage many further excursions, making the excuse that she knew he wanted to organize his camp before Alexander Zarras arrived.

She explored the narrow goat-trails

that wound up the harsh mountain-side, and glimpsed the wild sturdy goats far above foraging the terrain for a meagre supply of food. Some of them roamed free, others were tended by curly-headed boys, who grinned widely at her, showing strong white teeth.

She met men and women astride donkeys, already laden with merchandise for the town, usually panniers full of vegetables or dried fish. She found a small house tucked away, sheltered from the elements and facing the sea. A man outside was making pottery. Huge amphora-shaped jars of red-clay for holding water, and bowls and jugs of all sizes.

He smiled and gestured her to examine his wares. There were rows and rows already fired, and standing in the hot sun waiting for buyers. His Greek was rapid, but she understood enough to know that he wanted four drachmas for a beautifully shaped jar. She bought it. It would be nice filled with geraniums.

The women working in the olive-groves stopped to stare the first time she passed, but after a while they watched for her and smiled and shouted a greeting. They would straighten their dark-clad backs and run work-worn hands over faces the colour and texture of wizened walnuts. They smiled their gap-toothed smiles and hitched their black head coverings more firmly and then turned back to their jobs.

The main road ran all around the island. It was just a glorified cart-track, very rutty in parts. It meandered away, branching inland when it felt like it. There was little traffic, an occasional ancient taxi, imported from the mainland at great expense.

Most of the villagers in the outlying cluster of houses were fishermen, and used handcarts called carozzi. As everyone was friendly, and very often related to each other, it was an easy matter to borrow his neighbour's carozzo. A few boasted a proper cart with a donkey to pull it, but most donkeys or mules carried everything in panniers for the roads were so steep in parts that they could not pull the extra weight.

Ariadne loved those solitary walks. It brought back all the glamour of her childhood. Unfortunately she found none of her old playmates. Many young people were lured to the mainland to find work. Slowly, the economy of Xanos was dying.

But the town of Xanos itself was thriving. There was still a marble quarry and a small fish factory. And now a few tourists were finding their way to Xanos. New tavernas had sprung up and there was a new hotel, stark and modern . . . the Hermes, owned by the Gavalas family . . .

Ariadne eyed it as she passed one morning. It looked as if it catered for the very wealthy. Its very new whiteness hurt her eyes. She had to admit it blended well with its surroundings. Red tiles, deeply channelled, would carry flood water efficiently. Wide windows with green shutters and overhanging green awnings gave a cool look. Bougainvillaea and scarlet hibiscus climbed up pillars with severe white archways between.

Oleanders with pink or white blossoms grew in tubs in the courtyard, and in one corner grew several plumbago trees. It was cool and inviting.

'Admiring our new hotel?' Ariadne whirled about, to look into a pair of the brightest blue eyes she had ever seen. They twinkled down at her, taking in the smooth dark hair and the startled glance. Ariadne gave an uncertain smile and then looked back at the fiercely white façade.

'It is beautiful, isn't it?' The question in her answer, was suddenly doubtful. Did he not think it beautiful? She turned and regarded him. 'Do you not like it?'

'Yes and no. Yes, because it is easy on the eye, but it could easily have been in Majorca or Nice, or anywhere else for that matter. No, because it is too big for Xanos. We do not need tourists on Xanos.'

'Oh! So you are one of those people who think the natives are spoilt if they get a few mod cons and have an easier life! I am surprised at you in this day and age.'

'Not so. There is a difference in living an unspoilt idyllic life, growing enough for simple needs, and having time to stand and stare . . . or enjoy a feast day, without worrying about losing a day's pay, to a life geared to pandering to tourists.'

'You don't like tourists?'

He smiled down at her, his dark face lit up into pleasant creases.

'I am sorry. I do not like tourists in the mass. Individuals, yes. Are you a tourist?'

'No. I am living here.'

He raised well-shaped black eyebrows in disbelief.

'Really? I was not aware of it. But I have just returned from Tinos, so it is understandable.'

18

'Why should it be? Do you have to know everything that goes on in Xanos?'

'I suppose not, but I like to. It is an ingrained habit.'

'An interfering habit, I should think!'

'Tsk, tsk. The English have an unfortunate habit of treading dangerous ground, something about angels, I recollect!'

Ariadne glared at him. This Greek should be put in his place! Interfering superior male piggery! She had not invited him to speak to her. She fumed inwardly and said sweetly.

'Fiye apo tho! Fiyete!' The man stared at her with renewed interest.

'Well, well, well, a Greek! And telling me to go away! And I thought you were English. So you have come back to the old homestead, hey? Whose family do you belong to? Let me look at you and guess.' He pulled her round to face the bright sun. 'Hm, could be the Pappadopolouses, but not wide enough cheekbones, or the Yiorgis?' She shook her head, and then he frowned. 'You remind me . . . ' and then he caught his breath. 'Of course, the Kavouras!' His eyes searched her face. 'You are Nina Kavouras' daughter. You are very like her.' He pushed her away from him and turned away.

'I have been told so, many times. My father is Professor Powis. He is here on an archaeological expedition.'

'Of course. The English Professor! I knew of the project for they sought permission.'

'Permission for what?'

'To excavate the Gavalas land.'

'Then you are . . . ?'

'Michael Gavalas, at your service. Now, as you so admire our hotel, will you permit me to show you around the gardens? The courtyard here, is obviously newly planted. The trees went in fully grown and the whole thing is like a stage set. I should like to show you the orange and lemon groves at the back, and the view out to sea.'

'Thank you. I did not know . . . I

am sorry I was rude and called you interfering. But I still think you were a little overbearing.'

'Let us not quarrel again. It is too nice a morning for that. Come, we go through this wrought-iron gate, and pass the kitchen-garden, and take this winding path to the orange and lemon groves. I think you will agree they are beautiful.'

Ariadne smelled the sharp scents of herbs, as they passed through the kitchen garden. It was a bouquet of mint and sage and coriander, and the distinctive smell of thyme and garlic. Bees hummed lazily, and she saw they were frequenting the white flowers of a ginger-tree.

'A honey flow. Stop and listen. Can you hear the high-pitched hum? Some of those worker-bees will work at top speed until they drop dead, knowing that the important work of the hive will go on. Wonderful, isn't it?'

'What is that sweet-scented flower over there? The bush that has the big juicy-looking greyish leaves?'

'You mean the clusters of mauve-blue flowers resembling African violets? They are the flowers of the borage plant. The flowers are used for garnishing, and in certain of our wines. The leaves are used for clearing the blood, and for salads. They have a cooling salty cucumber-like taste, rather prickly and must be chopped finely.'

'You seem to know a lot about herbs, or are you just interested in good food?'

'I am a doctor. And I believe in herbs rather than drugs. That is why our herb garden is extensive. We grow foxgloves for digitalis. There are beds of fennel, dill and chervil over there, and others too numerous to mention; some you will not have heard of. The soil has been specially manufactured and mixed carefully to produce the best results. I have a laboratory here too.'

'It all sounds very fascinating. I should like to see it sometime.'

'So you shall. But we must not

talk shop all day. Come and see the groves.' The path wound past other oleanders, but these looked as if they had been growing for years. There were osiers and squat corob trees, and then she could smell the sharp scent of citrus fruit. It came stronger as they walked towards the groves. The black volcanic soil was carefully tilled, and black-clothed figures could be seen, bent over weeding, and spraying and pruning.

There were flowers and green fruits on the trees. Some were already ripening. As the summer sun grew hotter, workers would be out every day to gather the oranges and lemons just at the right stage.

It was cooler in the groves and they walked on until the path brought them out onto a natural plateau. The view was breathtaking.

'But this is wonderful!' Ariadne's lips curved in pleased surprise. Michael's eyes were drawn to her face. He moved closer.

'You see how the bay curves? From here, one can see as far as the island of Andros that way. See, the smudge on the sky-line to your left. And on your right, on a clear day one can see a hint of Siros. Hiros is just a little to the right of it. It is uninhabited, a bird sanctuary, but pleasant to visit for a picnic.'

'And what is the little island called, nestling in the bay not far from the shore?'

'Do you not know? That is Xanos's special own island. Our holy island.'

'I was only eleven when I was here last. There are certain aspects of the island I have forgotten. I do not remember that island.'

'That is Demeter Island. No one goes there. It is a holy place. There are the ruins of a temple on Demeter. A long forgotten place, now that the Orthodox or Catholic religion is practised. The followers of Apollo and Demeter, the Goddess of Fertility are all dead and gone. But the taboos are respected.

Besides, one can sail right round Demeter, and not find anywhere to land a boat. The cliffs are sheer and inaccessible.'

'It sounds rather a grim place. How did the worshippers land, then? There must have been a way.'

'Legend has it that there was a causeway across to the island which was later destroyed by earthquakes. A tunnel was then excavated, and used for thousands of years. The temple was a lookout for marauders. The islands have been overrun many times by Phoenecians, Romans and Spartans and many more have left their bloodstock behind. But to get back to Demeter. There is a way by sea. When the tide is at its height for about one hour, a flat-bottomed caique can land on a little plateau that faces Xanos.'

'And it has been done?'

'Yes, it has been known. Some of our oldest men recall landings on Demeter.'

'But what of the tunnel. Is it still used?'

'I do not think it still exists. Quakes and time will have destroyed it. If there is an entrance anywhere, the location must be surely lost.'

'A pity. It sounds so romantic. That glare of white on the island I can see, is that the temple?'

'Yes. Legend has it that the temple and the island were the most beautiful in the world. The temple was of a whiteness unsurpassed elsewhere and the grain of the marble the most sought after in those times. It could be seen far out to sea. Many ships were lost because they thought they could land, and they broke their backs on the hidden rocks.'

'You said Demeter was the Goddess of Fertility.'

'Yes. It is said she was born on the spot where the temple was built, just as Apollo was born on Delos. This island was hers and dedicated to all living things. Women would make the journey to pray for a child if they were barren. Farmers and fishermen prayed for good harvests, and they all took gifts.'

'It must have been a moving sight.'

'And then came a traitor who found the secret of the island, and the priests and priestesses were slain, and the temple destroyed, but as it was destroyed it also took the victors.'

'Whatever do you mean?'

'The meltemi wind sprang up. Some of the enemy's galleyships were lifted high and dry on the rising water and embedded on the rocks. The tide was highest it had ever been. The water pounded the ships to matchwood, and the undertow of the sea was so strong it washed away part of the foundations. The temple walls cracked and many pillars fell, killing priests and soldiers alike. A few lucky ships got away laden down with men fished out of the water. Others perished, or were washed off the rocks as the tide subsided. It is said the High Priest cursed all strangers that stepped ashore on Demeter, for all time.'

'But how do you know all this? Are there records?'

'A handful of soldiers did manage to get back to Xanos. They lived and died there. Writings and carvings have been found, and in the temple your father is now interested in, certain tablets and stones carved with pictures were found. They are now in the Museum in Athens.'

'It all seems so unreal, now here in the sun. It all looks so peaceful. Just like Paradise. Can I take a last peep? Can one see down below? I must look.'

Before he realized her intention, she darted forward to look over the cliff. The loose shaly rock slipped under her careless feet and she stumbled. She was grabbed with furious hands.

'You little fool! Don't ever try anything like that again!' He shook her in his emotion, his face a curious white under the deep tan. 'Your mother . . .'

He pulled her back to a safe distance but held her. She saw the fright and pain in his eyes. Then he pulled her to him and she was shaking with reaction. For one split second she had seen the restless water churning over the rocks far below. She felt faint but the hard arms encircling her did not slacken. She felt safe. And was that a butterfly kiss on the top of her head, or was it just imagination?

Embarrassment gave way to fear. She pushed him away, and silently started back along the path. They spoke no words, she, still shaken, and he, absorbed in his own thoughts. Then she stopped in the middle of the path.

'You mentioned my mother. Did you know her?'

'Yes, I knew Nina Kavouras. She was the reason I left Xanos.'

2

After lunch with her father, Ariadne went with him to the site. Alexander Zarras was expected to land from the mainland at about four o'clock, so the Professor wanted to make sure everything was ready for him.

The camp was to be divided into two separate projects, with mutual help from both sides if asked for, Elias Haralambas to become adviser for both parties. Stephanos Papitsis was to be in charge of the gold-seeking expedition, and Professor Powis would take charge and carry on work that had been started more than ten years ago.

They had recruited some local labour for the rough digging and removal of the sparse soil and rubble. The delicate monotonous work of the dig was assigned to Stavros and Petros, their youthful enthusiasm making light of the patient drudgery involved. They would offset boredom with songs both comic and patriotic, and would leap into one of the traditional shoulder-hugging dances at the first twang of a balalaika.

Miss Fafoutis would purse her lips and stare over the top of her huge spectacles disapprovingly. Then laughingly persuaded by the two young men, would throw caution aside, and dance with surprisingly gay abandon. Her chignon would come loose and her long hair would fall in a mist around her shoulders. Then panting and exhausted, she would pile up her hair and go back to her cataloguing . . .

The first time it happened, both Stephanos and Alexander Zarras gave her a second considering look, and certainly Alexander saw what lay behind those frightful glasses. He was now firmly installed and they were all one big happy family.

But this first afternoon, Ariadne found herself busy with tape-measure and note-pads and all the paraphernalia for marking out a new site. She was busy with her father when Elias came across to them with a stranger. Looking up at their approach, Ariadne stared at the new man. She heard the jumble of voices as her father shook hands, but her mind and heart were on the most beautiful face she had ever seen.

Dazed by the impact, she barely acknowledged the introduction, and felt further confusion at the firm hand-grip and the look in the tawny-brown eyes fringed with the longest lashes she had seen on a man. His smile was the reaction of a man well-used to the impact he had on women. It was his right and he expected it.

The crisp curly locks lifted in the slight breeze and were of a most unbelievable gold. The combination of hair and tawny eyes and deep tan were irresistible . . . It was not fair, thought Ariadne incredulously, that one man should have so much!

Then out of the welter of emotions,

a name sprang out. Gavalas! Paulo Gavalas! He held her hand a shade too long, giving it an intimate little squeeze. With an effort she drew back.

'Gavalas. I met someone of that name this morning. A Doctor Michael Gavalas.' She was suddenly doubtful. 'But he did not look like you. A tall, rather formidable man . . . and dark. We met near the Hermes Hotel.'

'My cousin,' he said casually. 'A worthy man, but a boor and no lady's man. It is a wonder he made your acquaintance. Were you by any chance admiring the hotel?'

'Looking at it. And wondering about it.'

'Ah, that explains it. He hates it, you know. My idea and my design. It belongs to me.'

'Are you joking? You really designed it?'

'Of course. I do not joke about a thing like that.' His face clouded over, and he appeared hurt and affronted, not the affable character of a moment ago. 'I trained as an architect, in Athens at the same time as Michael was a medical student. My father was alive then and living here in our villa in the interior.'

'Everyone has heard of the fabulous Villa Spyros,' said Elias. 'While we are speaking of it, I should like permission to look around. I understand it stands on a much older site.'

'It does. But visitors are not encouraged. It is a private residence, and will remain as such.' He spoke coldly, and Ariadne felt some sympathy for the crest-fallen Elias.

'I am sorry. I was only interested because of the great age. I meant no offence . . . ' He turned away, but not before Ariadne noted the dull red flush.

Professor Powis broke in, to pour oil on troubled waters.

'We must thank you for permission to return to this site. Your father was very good allowing us to start so many years ago. There was much found here at the time, but our survey was never completed.'

'I remember. There was some unpleasantness . . . I came here for a few weeks during the dig. We never met, but my father did tell me of your finds.'

Professor Powis's face had clouded over.

'Yes, it was most interesting at the time. The site does not appear to have been disturbed. But after my wife died . . . '

'Ah yes. Now I recall . . . Most remiss of me. I had forgotten. Please say no more.' He turned away, and then pointed to a strata of rock. 'I have reason to believe that is a marble bed, and stretches to nearly a mile inland. It should be investigated.' His voice receded as they made their way around the excavations.

She watched him go, fascinated and yet repelled. He was so different from his cousin Michael. He had engendered a feeling of antagonism, mainly because of his very masculinity. This man was an enigma. She turned away, disturbed and thoughtful.

But now, a certain routine had emerged. She breakfasted with her father, and then he left her to her own devices to go straight to the dig, which left much time on her hands.

Sometimes she joined the whole team at lunch time. The meal consisted of crusty bread, goat's cheese and salad, or perhaps grilled fish, or newly caught shrimps prepared by Yani, one of the casual labourers who volunteered to cook. He did so on open ground with rough spits and flat stones. When everything was ready he would bang a tin can and everyone would lay down tools and come running.

Then followed a siesta, through the hottest part of the day, with two or three hours working at night. Then, everyone relaxed and would converge on Babi's Taverna, to drink retsina, and the local rough wine, helped out with a handful of almonds or locally dried raisins.

Then, thoroughly relaxed, they would have dinner, which usually started with karpouzi (water-melon), fish or meat, souvlakia, small squares of meat grilled on skewers, or keftedes, tasty meat-balls done with succulent herbs. Huge salads were served with tomatoes, olives, cucumber and paprika, and followed by curd tarts, grapes and bitter-sweet coffee . . .

It was then, that Petros and Stavros came into their own. They would join the local revellers, and each night was party night. At first they would give their own, rather more sophisticated floor show, and then the locals would join in, and they would show what they could do. They danced and whirled to the beat of the three local musicians, and even the old men joined them.

There was no formality. A man wanting to dance would just join the line of dancers. When he tired, he just dropped out, but the dancing went on.

At first, Ariadne found it all exciting. It brought back memories of other nights, sitting with Mother and Father, one at each side of her. And she had glimmers of memory of her mother laughing and dancing, and singing to a balalaika. She could remember her plucking the strings. Where was that instrument now?

The first time she slipped out of the taverna for a quiet walk along the stony beach, she did it because she had a headache. After that she did it for pleasure. It was much more agreeable to sit on an upturned boat and listen to the music from a distance. She would gaze out at the moon-speckled water, and her eyes and her thoughts would turn to the little island, glowing in the dark of a navy-blue sea.

It was as if this island of Xanos was reaching out to her. It, and the small island of Demeter were so steeped in legend, that something left over from the past was trying to weave some kind of strange enchantment . . .

Or was it all due to the people of the island? The fisherfolk and their tales of water-gods, and their rituals before putting out to sea? Or the farmers who still talked of Demeter as the great earth-mother? And above all, the strange Gavalas cousins?

For wherever Ariadne went, someone would speak of the Gavalas family. Some spoke with admiration. Their wealth and power on the island were impressive, and few villagers would care to offend them . . . But some spat contemptuously, stealthily, after looking both ways. They, with closed faces and sullen looks would hurry away, muttering about work to do. It was all very exasperating . . .

Ariadne was just making her mind up one night to seek out her father and retire to the Mykonos Hotel for the night, when a foot scraping on the shingle disturbed her. Glancing up, she saw Michael Gavalas looking down at her.

'Hello, all alone? May I sit down for awhile?'

'I was just thinking about moving. My father . . . '

'Stay awhile, and talk to me. How do you like Xanos now you have got settled in?'

'Very much, thank you. I felt as if I was coming home when I first arrived. Everyone is so friendly.'

'Of course, you will have relatives on the island. You are one of us.'

'I don't think so. Dad did not mention relatives.'

'Has he not? That is strange. Nina Kavouras had a sister Marigoula who lived on the other side of the island, and a mother. Her father died at sea many years ago.'

Ariadne was taken aback. Why had her father never mentioned her mother's sister and her mother? Strange! Never once had she ever considered the possibility of having Greek relatives!

'Do you know them? And where they live?'

Michael shrugged. 'I knew Marigoula years ago, but I have only been back on the island for five years. I do not meet everybody. Perhaps they still live in the old fisherman's cottage near Kamari, the only other large town on the island.'

'I must ask Dad about them. I may even be able to visit . . . '

'Perhaps you should wait, before making plans,' he said gravely. 'I may have spoken out of turn. Your father may have a reason for not acknowledging them.'

'But that's absurd! What reason could he have?' Michael shrugged again.

'The Kavouras family are very proud. Some Greeks do not like the idea of marrying outside their own community. But I am only guessing. Come, let us walk awhile and I shall point out the stars to you.'

'No.' She whirled around. 'You said you knew my mother. Why did you say you left Xanos on her account?'

41

He sat very still. She just caught his intake of breath. She glanced at him but his face was half in shadow. She waited. The silence grew longer . . . She stirred uneasily. Then he spoke.

'It was a long time ago. I knew her as a spirited young girl who loved the sea. She sailed her father's boat and sometimes helped him when he was hired to take his boat out for a day's fishing. I was brought up in Athens, and only occasionally visited my uncle and cousin. My aunt was dead, and my uncle's housekeeper had the bringing up of Paulo . . . He was a strange solitary boy, so my visits were encouraged.' He stopped and looked out to sea, as if lost in his own thoughts. Then he continued. 'We had a boy and girl affair for one long hot summer. It was all very innocent. Looking back, it was too idyllic to last. We quarrelled and I left Xanos and did not return for several years. I became a medical student, and I suppose the memory of Nina faded, as it usually does with young people. That's all there was to it.'

He made it sound very casual, but Ariadne wondered . . . Nina had meant very much to him, she did not doubt. Whether it was her woman's intuition or not, she felt his underlying emotions. Dare she ask what they had quarrelled about? But one look at the dark, shadowed face, changed her mind. He had a right to his privacy. It was too late to probe. Nothing good could come of it.

'Thank you for telling me.' She stood up and held out her hand. 'It is not often I can talk about my mother. Dad always seems reluctant to talk about her. I think he must still miss her badly. I must go now, he will wonder where I am.'

They walked together back to the door of the taverna. It faced the sea, and Petros and Stavros were still singing. Michael took her hand in his for a moment.

'Thank you for listening to me. I

may see you another evening.' Before she could reply, he had gone.

Several days passed and she saw nothing of Michael or Paulo. Once, a white Mercedes streaked past just as she was coming to a cross-roads. Paulo was staring ahead and did not see her. She was both relieved and sorry. She could not understand herself.

She visited Katerina Pappadopolous and her daughter Annalika, her husband Takis being busy down in the little harbour. They drank fragrant lemon tea in the old drystone-walled garden, amidst tamarisks and an ancient gnarled grapevine which ran the whole length of the house wall.

Katerina was very pleased at the visit, considering it an honour. Her broad face beamed.

'Try some of our almond cakes. Our own almonds, ground fresh, and mixed with our own honey. Very nice!'

Ariadne beamed her thanks. She turned to Annalika, who was a shy girl and needed drawing out. Ariadne asked her about her engagement and found out that they were already preparing the brides' clothes and collecting the dowry.

'And Leonardou has already had a cottage promised. One of O-Kirios Gavalas' cottages.'

'Mr. Gavalas' cottages? Which Mr. Gavalas?'

'There is only one O'Kirios Gavalas, Mr. Paulo. He owns most part of the island. Mr. Michael is a yatrós, doctor. He lives with Mr. Paulo, but it is said he left a good practice to live with him.'

'Why should he do that? Why leave a good practice?'

'I do not know.' Annalika looked at her mother who was busy cutting a bunch of grapes. 'Some say he lives as a parasite on Mr. Paulo's generosity. My mother gets angry when she hears what is said. Yatrós Michael saved my father's life when he was injured in his boat during a storm. Neither will hear a word said against him.'

'But I thought they would be popular around here, especially when they employ so much labour. And the new hotel will attract more tourists. Surely they will bring more business to Xanos?'

'The older people do not want tourists. Neither does Yatrós Michael. It is said high words were spoken on the subject of more tourists. But who is he to lay down the law? He is only a hanger-on after all!'

'Why does Mr. Paulo not send Michael away? Surely, if he does not want Michael there he could send him away?'

Annalika looked around at her mother who was busy examining her vine.

'It is said Yatrós Michael blackmails Mr. Paulo. I do not think it is true. For Yatrós Michael is a good man. But as you say, why does not Mr. Paulo send him away?'

'Why do you talk of blackmail?' Annalika shrugged.

'I do not. It is but villagers' gossip.

46

If they do not understand they make up their own reasons. But Michael stays, and does nothing. He lives a life of ease, and only helps the local doctor on very few occasions. Everyone is suspicious of him. So why stay?'

3

The vexed question of why Michael stayed, bothered Ariadne quite some time. She had plenty of time on her hands and she was bored. There was little to do, and after walking so many times along the same paths, they lost their charm. But the climb to the top of the cliffs never palled. She found a new ascent after walking past several box-like houses set well back in niches, sheltering from the wind. The way was winding, and sometimes only negotiable by steps cut into the rock. It took quite some time to reach the top, but the view was worth it.

The panorama of sea and cliffs and clustering houses in the bay was breathtaking. Far more could be seen than from down below at the Hermes Hotel. She could see Syros and Andros much clearer. In fact, she could see Mount Syringas on Syros. It appeared purple-greyish in a rearing hazy mass above the horizon. She would sit for hours, and wonder at the beauty of it all.

Afterwards, she could never remember why she started to explore that particular part, but by accident she found another path that ran round behind a huge boulder. She thought it was just another goat-path but surprisingly, it widened as it ran slopingly downhill again.

It meandered away from the white box-like houses and disappeared into a deepening cleft. Overhanging boulders nearly met overhead, and caused deep purple shadows. It was used, that was certain. Fresh donkey tracks and occasional imprints of footwear could be seen. Wherever it led, she was sure it would eventually come out somewhere near the town.

Before she plunged into the shadows, she paused to look at the view. She appeared to be in the middle of the arc of the bay. The sparkling blue of the water, turning turquoise nearer the outer rocks and then to dark green where the shadows lay, dazzled her eyes. White foam like lace swirled about and edged the bay with movement. She could make out the main street and Takis Pappadopolous's house and pocket-handkerchief garden. She could not see the Mykonos Hotel. It was out of her vision, but the Hermes was easily recognizable, and there was a white Mercedes drawn up outside . . . To the right, a little of the old temple of Apollo was visible, the remains of cracked pillars jutting out like broken teeth midst scrubby grass and smothering weed. Thousands of years ago, it would have stood proud, facing the sea. A long line of glowing white marble pillars with an angled roof and probably statues of Apollo and Demeter, beckoning the mariners into the harbour. It would have been a landmark, well-known and looked for. Now, a heap of rubble, all that was left after some distant great catastrophe, just another site for her father to probe and excavate, and wrest from it the long-lost secrets of a much earlier civilization. She passed into the shadows and on between the boulders. The path narrowed to a donkey's width. Then the trail widened and she was blinking again in strong sunlight.

She had stumbled into a hidden valley. Down below she could see the shattered marble pillars of a temple. The marble was creamy with dark veins running through it. There was a hint of green about it, as if it were covered with mould. Scrubby reeds and grasses grew up round and through the decaying heaps.

Slithering and sliding she managed to climb down the path of loose shale, without any hurt. Walking easily was a difficulty. Her heart beat fast. Perhaps her father would find clues here of an earlier civilization. She wondered why it appeared to be unknown and deserted.

Skirting the site, she realized it had

been a small temple, probably of some lesser deity. There was a hint of scrolls and carving. Whoever had built it had been an expert architect, employing only the best craftsmen.

She climbed up some crumbling steps onto a smooth mosaic floor. Most of the mosaics had long gone, but fragments remained to hint at its beauty. A pile of rubble attracted her, and she crossed the floor to examine it further. She stood up on the stump of a smooth pillar to look down on the rest. This was an easy matter as several smaller pieces made a rough staircase.

Amazed, she stared down at what was most certainly the remains of a Collossus . . . Yes, there was a broken arm, with a weathered hand. A huge foot planted firmly in a marble bed and the torso of a man, without his head.

She scrambled down and worked her way round the huge mass, intent on locating the head. It was as she thought, a little way farther on, still in the same position to which it had rolled all those years ago.

Climbing and scrambling, she managed to stand beside it and pulled away the encroaching grasses. It was Apollo, his sightless eyes gazing up to heaven. But what made her catch her breath was the likeness! The hair, the shape of the nose and face. It was Paulo Gavalas caught forever in marble!

Fascinated, she looked at it from all angles. Then she shivered. It was uncanny. She turned to leave this place, that suddenly seemed menacing.

'What are you doing here?' A harsh voice split the silence. She looked up and saw Paulo Gavalas. For a moment she hardly recognized him. His face seemed contorted and twisted. Probably a trick of the light, she thought afterwards.

Then recognizing her, he was himself in an instant. He jumped down from the high promontory he was standing on and came to her side.

'I'm sorry, I seem to be trespassing. It was not intended.'

Paulo smiled.

'I was startled and angry when I saw the figure. It was unexpected. There is a notice farther on. This is private land, you know.'

'Then I shall go. I shall not trespass in future!' She turned to go the way she came.

'Wait! I want to talk to you. Besides, that way is bad walking. To climb up again would be nearly impossible.'

'I could manage. I am no weakling, you know,' she said tersely.

'Now you are offended. I am sorry. Am I forgiven? I thought you were some nosy villager . . . '

'If I were, what harm could I have done? I was only looking, and was very surprised to find this temple . . . to Apollo, isn't it?'

'Yes. You are very astute. What do you think of it? My very own temple.' His face was proud and eager. He really wanted to know. A strange man, this Paulo Gavalas!

'I suppose it must have been very

impressive once. And I was looking at the face of Apollo . . . '

'Yes? And what did you think?' For a moment there was a look of exultation on his face.

'I thought . . . I know it sounds silly, but there was a look of you. At least, you look like him.'

'So you see it too! Do you know much about the Greek Gods?'

'A little. I was interested at school.'

'You know about Hermes and Athens, Artemis and Demeter, Goddess of Fertility? And how Apollo took many guises? He is Apollo Karnaios to the shepherds, protector of flocks; Phoebus Apollo, God of Divine Radiance, protector of human reason and lucidity of mind and Lizard-Slayer Extraordinary. He fostered the arts of medicine and was champion of the Arts and Sciences.'

'You make him sound like a Saint. He had his dark side as well! He hurled plagues at his enemies, and he was merciless in his fury!'

'Ah, so you have studied Apollo! A good friend and bad enemy. You remind me . . . ' He fell silent. Then he said, 'Come, I will give you a rough idea of the layout. This place actually was what you would call in England, the lodge at the gate at the approach to a country mansion.'

'How in the world do you make that out? The only other temple on Xanos, is the one my father is excavating, the old Minoan temple, and it lies on the other side of the town.' Paulo smiled secretively and then shrugged.

'Perhaps so. But as I said, it is a lodge. Apollo guarding his most prized possession. Look, here is the altar, where the huge Collossus would stand. Over there, and there, are the side altars to other lesser Gods. The rows of pillars here . . . and here,' he pointed, absorbed in recreating the temple in his mind, 'covered over with huge slabs carved with cherubs and scrolls. And the avenue for musing priests and priestesses. Can you imagine the scene in its hey-day. The glory of it, and the dedication, and above all, the exultation of *being* that God Apollo?' Ariadne looked puzzled.

'But Apollo wasn't really a man. He was a deity, a legend, a figure sculpted in marble. You make him sound . . . '

'Of course he was no ordinary man!' Paulo interrupted impatiently. 'He was one of the Immortals that walked this earth in a more enlightened age, where Gods were concerned. But he lived and loved and suffered on Olympus. Ah, if only those days could return!'

He was stroking the foot of the great Collossus as he spoke. He appeared abstracted and strange. Ariadne felt a sudden fear. Did Paulo suffer from delusions? But that was nonsense. It was her highly excitable imagination at work. Paulo was only steeped in local legends. Being born and bred on the island, and being very sensitive, it was only natural the legends of the Gods might creep into his every-day life. And yet . . .

Uneasily, she made a move.

'I must be going. My father will worry. Can I get back to Xanos if I keep following this path downwards?' Paulo seemed to struggle with himself, and his rather blank eyes re-focussed on her. He smiled sweetly, banishing the past and concentrating on the present. He looked at her closely.

'Yes, yes,' he said impatiently. 'The path leads back to Xanos. Do you know you are very like her?' He stepped closer and tipped up her chin with a gentle finger. 'Yes, very like. It is extraordinary.' Ariadne dared not breathe. She wanted to move away from him but something stopped her. His finger traced her jawline and then moved to her neck. She felt his hand caress her and his thumb ran up and down her windpipe and gently press.

'Who am I like?' She could only whisper. She tried to back away but he held her.

'Demeter, my Goddess who came back to me, only to escape me by falling over that cliff at that point, there!' He pointed to a jutting headland. 'Come, I'll show you where it happened.' He pulled her forward. 'Or perhaps you know. Perhaps you *are* Demeter. Destined to keep returning for all time, to scourge, mock and torment me. Are you?' His hand tightened around her neck until there was a singing in her ears.

'Paulo!' The shout was authoritative and full of menace. Paulo started and his hand relaxed. Ariadne, coughing and choking, sank down onto a slab of marble.

Michael took in the situation at a glance, bounded down the loose shale and panting came to a halt beside them. He lifted Ariadne up and supported her.

'Are you all right? Has he hurt you?' Ariadne shook her head. Her throat ached, but apart from that she was unhurt. Paulo had returned to his usual gentle self.

He looked down at Ariadne as if

59

someone else had molested her, and with as much concern.

'My poor dear Ariadne, what a shocking thing to happen! I have had notices put up forbidding access to this place. It can be dangerous, you know!' Ariadne remained dumb. It was all taking on a dream-like quality.

'Paulo, you had no right to come here like this. You promised me it wouldn't happen again! How dare you go back on your word?' Michael spoke roughly, controlled anger ready to break.

'Stop it, Michael! Who are you to tell me what to do? I'll come and go as I please. I only took a walk to get away from that damned house. I was suffocating in there. Then I saw someone I thought was an intruder. I came to order her off the property and recognized her. That is all there is to it.'

'I wish to God that that was all! Do you realize what you nearly did?' Paulo turned sharply away.

'Forget it, Michael. She is none the

worse for her experience. I got a little carried away, that's all. I would not have harmed her. It will teach her to keep away from this place.'

'Go home, Paulo. I shall take Ariadne back to Xanos.'

'Yes you do that. She was asking about the way into Xanos. It is better for her to have an escort, one never knows who is lurking about.' He smiled down at her as if nothing had happened. 'I'll do as you say, Michael. I have a headache.' He turned to go. Laughing, he ran up the narrow cliff path and turned to wave and then he was gone.

Ariadne turned to face Michael. His face was grim as he watched Paulo disappear along the path. Then his face changed and softened as he examined her throat. There was the slightest of blue marks.

'You must forgive Paulo. When he is in one of his exalted moods, he really forgets he is just a mortal man, and that other people can be hurt.'

'Has he done this kind of thing before?'

Michael hesitated. 'There was some talk of a girl . . . He sighed. 'It all happened a long while ago . . . while I was in Athens, and before my Uncle died. It was an unpleasant episode with a village girl. I thought he was getting much better.'

'You mean you are here to look after him?'

'In a way. My uncle was never sure of him. And there was your mother . . . I was away at the time. My uncle successfully suppressed all connection with her, but I suspect there was something. Paulo loved your mother, I am sure of that.'

'You think he killed her? Or drove her to suicide?'

'I am not saying that. It could have been an accident. But one doesn't go over a cliff very easily, especially when one knows those cliffs from childhood. Now this has happened, it has awakened fears that Paulo is not quite . . . normal.'

'Can you do anything for him?' Ariadne could feel nothing but pity for Paulo, whose beauty of face belied his hidden weakness, and for Michael who shouldered the full weight of responsibility for him.

'Until he shows any further abnormality, I can do nothing. He is his own master. But my uncle warned me. I thought he was being over-dramatic. Now I am not so sure. Are you feeling better? Can you tackle the footpath? We can take it easy and talk as we go.'

'Yes. I'm not badly hurt, you know. I was frightened and shocked. It came out of the blue, and the idea of Paulo doing such a thing was appalling . . . ' She shuddered.

'Please forget it. I do not really think he had any real thoughts of hurting you.'

They proceeded down the path and Michael took her hand to help her. He was gentle and kind and she felt truly safe. She pondered and then said slowly.

'He was confused. He mixed me up with Demeter, his Goddess. He said I had come back, only to be lost again. I don't understand the allusion.'

'That damned housekeeper is to blame. My uncle left him too much alone. The local children were not good enough for him to play with, and old Anyah spoilt him and filled his head with wild ideas. From early childhood, Uncle spent much of his time on the mainland and Paulo was quietly indoctrinated. I have heard it said that Paulo roamed the hills as a young teenager, calling on the old Gods to give him a sign. Takis Pappadopolous was so disturbed at the rumours he personally wrote to my uncle, begging of him to return and restrain him.'

'Poor Paulo. He must have led a lonely introverted life.'

'Yes, and still does. The villagers believe he has the evil eye, and shun him. The reason he had the huge hotel built, was to attract tourists and create for himself a new society.'

'Michael, many people think you are a parasite, living on your cousin's bounty. I do not believe this, but I do not like hearing it. Can you not stop this scurrilous talk?'

He laughed. 'I know what the villagers think. I don't really care. How can I tell the world I live on Xanos to watch over my eccentric cousin? So I let them talk. But you don't know how pleased I am that you did not believe all that rubbish . . . Ariadne . . . look at me.'

He turned her abruptly to face him, and for a moment their glances locked. Something in his eyes set her heart racing. His head came down and his lips touched hers gently, and then an engulfing flame enveloped them both and they clung together in a rising tide of passion. She felt him tremble and then he thrust her away and looked again into her eyes.

'Forgive me, Ariadne. I took you by

surprise. Thank you for being so sweet.'
He squeezed her shoulders beneath
gentle hands and lightly kissed her nose.
She felt suddenly bereft. Was it just
reaction after that other unpleasantness,
on her part? Was he just being grateful
for her belief in him? It appeared so.
But for herself, the day had dulled and
depression had set in.

She followed him along the rocky
path and he was careful to help her
over the rough patches, but after doing
so, relinquished her hand. It was as if
he was deliberately pushing her away.

They came to an easy smooth path,
rather more on the level. It broadened
and wound round a huge boulder.
At the other side Ariadne stopped in
amazement. Under the huge boulder
ran a subterranean stream. It reminded
Ariadne of a huge black face with open
mouth from which poured a spout of
water.

Michael watched the expressions
come and go on the mobile face. A
little smile touched his mouth.

'I knew you would be surprised. Everyone is the first time they see it. It is one of the few springs on the island and it starts way back at the top of the mountain. It is a great sight after a storm. The water tumbles and boils and flings itself down to the sea.'

'It is a beautiful sight, and look, a little further down it seems to run over a ledge. A real waterfall, in fact!'

'Yes. It drops, as you can see, about thirty foot, and no man can swim in the cauldron at the bottom. There is a whirlpool and everything is sucked down. Watch!'

They descended to the nearest spot overlooking the fall. Michael threw a dead branch into the leaping, wildly rushing spray. The current caught it and it whirled round and round and then it just disappeared.

'Look! Did you see it go?' shouted Michael in her ear. The roar of the water at that point made talking difficult. She nodded, and they walked on. She looked back when they were a safe distance away.

'It is awe-inspiring. And makes one feel so small. Does it all directly flow into the sea as a river? I don't seem to remember a river-mouth along the coast.'

'No. It goes underground again through what the locals call Pluto's mouth. According to legend, the water goes to keep all growing things alive until the great awakening, when Persephone is allowed by Pluto to once more walk the earth with her mother, Demeter, mother of the Earth and Goddess of Fertility. In the old days, offerings were thrown into the 'mouth' to ensure a bountiful harvest. It was said that the river ran right to Demeter's own temple on the holy island. Look, it is directly ahead from here.'

Ariadne shaded her eyes and so it was, a glittering romantic place, lonely, and waiting . . . She shook herself. She was becoming fanciful. This island, with its aura of age and legend plucked at her reason. She was no longer sure of herself. Was everyone affected in the same way? Was the island to blame for Paulo's obsession and what about Michael?

She turned slowly, and her eyes were beseeching.

'Michael . . . ' She held out a shy tentative hand. He ignored it and turned away.

'Don't,' he grated. 'I should never have kissed you. I never meant . . . '

'Why? Michael, why?' Pain over-shadowed shyness. She clung to his hand and brought it up to her lips. 'Was that only an impulse on your part, or was it something else? And if it was something else, why repulse me?'

'Because I am Paulo's cousin and his blood is my blood,' he said harshly. 'I'm a doctor, remember? And I know all about heredity and the misery a canker can cause.' He caught her to him in a passionate embrace. 'By God, never think I don't love you! I think of you night and day, but I cannot let you become embroiled in the curse of the Gavalas family!'

'I don't care! It's you I love, not Paulo, or the Gavalas family!'

'My sweet, you have no idea what you are talking about! For one thing, you have not known me long enough. You want to rush into a situation you cannot gauge, all because you enjoyed my company and my kiss. Besides . . . I am years older than you. I was in love with your mother, remember?'

'Age doesn't mean a thing. I love you, Michael, really love you. I shall not change.'

'But you must. Life is all change. What you think at twenty, is an anathema at thirty. I haven't the right to love anybody, Ariadne. Don't you understand?'

'I only understand you don't want my love.' She broke away from him and ran, hair flying and feet stumbling down to the little road that lay ahead. A sob caught in her throat. All she wanted to do was to run back to the

Mykonos Hotel and fling herself on her bed and cry her eyes out . . .

Michael watched her go, with pain and pity in his heart. How could he tell her of what lay in his heart? The black shadow that had almost wrecked his life? The thing that had driven him on in the first place to become a doctor? How twin brothers could hate each other so much that after each had a son, they had both tried to murder the other! Insanity stalked the Gavalas family. He was determined that the family should die out, with himself and Paulo being the last of the strain. Paulo, he suspected, had difficulty with women . . . He would be no problem that way. At forty-three, he could live out his life, if carefully watched. It was his duty to see that nothing untoward happened, even though all his instincts wanted him to return to medicine . . . Of his own yearnings with regard to Ariadne, he closed his heart. She was only twenty and had all her life before her. He was eighteen years older, and, he hoped, mature enough to put away all thoughts of love.

Sadly he turned and made his way back to the Villa Spyros, the Gavalas home for many generations. He stood for awhile before entering the ornate main gate, decorated with cherubs, snakes and various flora and fauna. He remembered it with love. So many happy hours spent there with Paulo and old Anyah. She had been like a mother to both of them.

Now he looked at the house with a stranger's eyes. It was whitewashed and glowing; the flamboyant lines of modern Greek architecture at its most expensive and best. The arches and columns were in traditional style and the dull weathered roof of tiles channelled to take a heavy downpour, came well over the windows to give as much shade as possible. The roof levels varied, and brick chimney-stacks gave character. Turrets at each end of the house put him in mind of a small fortress. Now, the whole had a neglected air. Twisting vines around pillars had not been pruned as in his uncle's day, and the huge jars of terracotta, not planted and tended as they should. The patio needed sweeping. Anyah was getting old and Paulo did not care.

Was this lovable old house, the scene of many childish escapades, to become his prison too? Were Paulo and he to become so closely entwined that neither should have any life apart? Was the curse of the twins, their fathers, to fall on them and were they destined to live their lives out, together?

Michael bent his head and walked on. Renunciation was much harder than he had ever imagined.

4

Unhappiness made Ariadne look for companionship amongst the excavation team. Professor Powis was surprised and delighted at her renewed interest. She offered to help Eugenie with the cataloguing and found it much more absorbing than she expected.

She found her interest centred mainly on the temple site itself, rather than on any finds. It was amazing how one could easily interpret the use of the excavated rooms. Bones of varied kinds were found in heaps, beside the remains of a huge chimney space, denoting the kitchen area of the priests' living quarters. There were still the marks of a pair of huge bronze doors that had opened and scraped the mosaic floor underneath the still standing lintel. How many people had walked backwards and forwards through those doors!

She could picture the leisurely walks along by the towering colonnades. The old priests walking, book in hand, and perhaps students following at a respectful distance. The lookouts in the watch-towers, awaiting the return of conquering heroes or watching for the first signs of enemy ships, and the faint sound coming over the water of the drums, beating out the time for the slaves shackled to the oars . . .

One morning Eugenie shut her ledger with a bang.

'You look tired, Ariadne. We are going to take the morning off. What do you say to a swim and a picnic? We *all* need a change. I was telling your father yesterday, we keep our noses to the grindstone too much.'

'A good idea. I've not been sleeping too well.'

'Anything wrong, dear? Can I do anything to help?'

'I don't think so, Eugenie. Thanks anyway. Just out of sorts, I guess. I've got past the holiday mood. When I first came here I was excited and felt as if I was coming home. I remembered Xanos with the mind of a child. The reality is very different. I feel restless, and half inclined to be homesick for London. Ridiculous really, when I dreamed of coming back here for so long!'

'Understandable and very human. Until now, you have had no real purpose here. It has been all holiday and now you are bored.'

Ariadne agreed, but her eyes were sad. She had seen no more of Michael. He had not sought her out again, and now, when she remembered her outburst she felt humiliated. How could she have been such a fool! All very well to tell her he loved her, but she had warned him off with her silly outpourings! He evidently regarded her as just a silly girl, easily influenced and ready to fall in love with the first man who kissed her.

A holiday romance! What must he

really think of her? Her cheeks burned. But for her it was no holiday romance. She knew he was right for her, and no silly fears on his part, and she was firmly convinced they were silly, would alter the fact. She even persuaded herself that Paulo's lapse had not really happened, that the unpleasantness was just an accident . . . a little horseplay, nothing else.

Stavros and Petros were keen on the idea of a picnic, and Professor Powis reluctantly agreed to go as well. There was a natural swimming pool farther along the coast, with deep caves for undressing. Yani and Eugenie went away together, to discuss food, leaving Ariadne with her father.

They were sitting companionably together drinking the local thirst-quenching drink of white wine, soda-water, a slice of lemon and ice from the gas-ice-box, when she remembered Marigoula and her grandmother.

'Dad, why did you never mention my aunt and grandmother?'

'What do you mean?' He turned to her, his usually pre-occupied eyes suddenly alert and keen.

'My mother's sister, Marigoula and her mother. Why do we not visit them?'

'Because they refused to have anything to do with us after Nina married me. It is a long story, Ariadne, and not altogether pleasant. The Kavouras family were proud and wild. I doubt if we should get a welcome, even after all these years.'

'But *why*? Surely they could not object to you? You loved each other. They could not expect more than that!'

'They were poor, but very proud. Your mother was a lovely girl, and they thought she had a chance of marrying one of the Gavalas cousins. If she had, the whole Kavouras family would have benefited. Uncles, cousins, brothers, sisters . . . you name them. They *all* expected advancement.'

'You mean it would have been Michael, rather than Paulo?'

'Yes. He spent a whole summer vacation at the Villa Spyros, and I understand they spent it together. But they quarrelled and he left suddenly. He was only a boy, much younger than your mother and, I think, jealous of her easy friendship with other men.'

'Then you were not the reason for the quarrel?'

'Oh no. I did not come to Xanos until a year later. I came out on a student grant. She was so alive and beautiful, I had no eyes for anyone else . . . The family expected Michael to return again, and they wanted to keep her for him. But he did not return again for years . . . Then there was talk of Paulo and her, but nothing came of it. It was said in the village, he did not like girls. I don't know.' He shook his head.

'Dad, was my mother easy?' He looked away, but not before Ariadne saw the hurt in his face.

'Darling, don't ask me that. I like to think not. She was a passionate girl, full of life and she could be very exhausting. She had a temper and would throw things when roused. I was a fool. I hated those violent exhibitions and expected her to live a quiet, ordered life like an Englishwoman. Now I see what a mistake it was . . . '

'Poor mother. I only remember the laughter, the petting and the sudden tears.'

'When you came along, it was the happiest time of my life. We left Xanos and went back to England where I completed my studies. She hated England, and life in Cambridge. She was choked and frustrated. So when I got the chance to go back to Xanos to work on the excavation of this temple I was pleased. She was wildly excited at the thought of going back . . . But it did not turn out as she expected. Her friends and relations did not want to know her.'

'Yes, I remember her crying and sobbing on the big double bed and me feeling frightened, and you were not there to comfort her, and I was angry with you.'

'You are right. I was not there, just when she needed me. I was in my own little world, immersed in my work, and God forgive me, I thought she was overacting as usual!'

'She was lonely, Daddy. Did you know that?'

'I realized it later. I thought you were enough for her. I loved her. She knew that, and I did not think it important enough to keep telling her. I took her for granted . . . '

'And she thought she came second to your work! Did she, Dad? Was Mother only second-best?'

'Yes.' The word seemed to be dragged out of him. His eyes appeared haunted. 'I should never have married her. I loved her passionately from first seeing her, but I never understood her. I dreaded her tantrums. I was too young to recognize the call for help or understanding. She picked quarrels, and I hated her for it. She disturbed my orderly way of life. Now I see she was trying to claim my attention, to make me aware of her. I was just a stupid unimaginative idiot, and so she turned to Paulo.'

'So that is why I remind Paulo of Demeter. Mother was his Demeter, and she escaped him, and now, I remind him of her.'

'I was not aware of the association until after the accident. Then of course, it all came out. The meetings, and the quarrels. Oh yes, even theirs was a stormy relationship. Someone testified at the inquest that there were many quarrels. And the night she died, she had taunted him with being half a man. But one youth swore that she slipped and fell. Another youth said they struggled together and Nina hit Paulo in the face. But that night there was a full moon, and it cast strange shadows, so no one could testify about what really happened. Paulo himself, said very little. He seemed wrapped up in himself. We left Xanos after the funeral, for I wanted to get you away to school and fill your mind with other things.'

'Oh Daddy, if only . . . '

'Do you think I haven't said that many times?' he said fiercely. 'I really did love her, Ariadne. And like a careless fool, I lost her.'

Eugenie came to them, all packed and ready to be away.

'My, you've had a long chat, the pair of you. Are you ready to move? Stephanos and Alexander will come along later. They are going to explore some of those deep caves and see if there is any sign of that gold. They are getting very despondent. They are both of the opinion that if gold was ever hidden on these islands, the Germans must have come back quietly and taken it away. All the clues seem to dissolve into thin air when investigated.'

'They have both worked hard, here and on the other islands,' said the Professor. 'I think the Government will give up if Zarras doesn't come up with a good idea soon.'

'Are you ready, Ariadne? Have you got your bikini with you?' said Eugenie. 'And you too Professor. You must have a dip. It will blow the cobwebs away.' Her warm brown eyes caught his, and Ariadne caught her breath. Surely Eugenie was taking a great interest in her father's welfare?

For a moment she was stunned, and then she considered. Her father was still a fine-looking man, quite a lot older than Eugenie, but they had a lot in common. Could it be possible . . . ? She smiled wryly. Who was she to match-make? She couldn't manage her own affairs!

But when they got to the stony beach of the little cove where the incoming tide swept into the natural pool, she was more certain than ever. Eugenie made her father comfortable. She consulted him as to the best place for the picnic, and poured him out his favourite drink. She sat beside him and talked in a more animated way, than

84

when she was merely working with him. This then, was the real Eugenie!

And Ariadne liked what she saw. Quietly, she moved over to one of the deep caves and changed into her swimsuit. She joined Petros and Stavros in the water. She was quite a strong swimmer, and as the tide was high, it just lapped the rocks which encircled the pool. There was no undertow, or pull and swimming was enjoyable and easy.

Petros waved and dived, and before she knew it, she was being pulled under. Gasping, she surfaced, and laughing went after him, but he was too good a swimmer for her to catch. Stavros however, watching the byplay, intervened and Ariadne and he managed to pull him up by his ankles and left him to flounder.

For awhile they played catch-as-catch-can and then Ariadne tired, and sat on the edge of the pool to watch a spectacular diving display by Stavros and Petros. Both were strong muscular boys, deeply tanned and handsome in their own way. Stavros, the taller of the two, was perhaps the quicker-tempered, but more outgoing. It was he who began the singing and dancing at night. Petros was gentle and merry, content to follow where Stavros led.

Now, they vied with one another to produce the most spectacular dive. Ariadne noticed Eugenie and her father, attracted by the laughter, come to the pool edge. They splashed happily in the shallows and Ariadne saw the look of strain disappearing from her father's face. She waved cheerily to Eugenie but did not attempt to go to them. It was best to let them spend their time alone together . . .

Alexander Zarras and Stephanos Papitsis joined them, and it was not long before they too were in the pool. But now, they joined the Professor and Eugenie. Their little interlude was over, and Ariadne saw with amusement, her father's ill-concealed irritation.

Alexander and Stephanos had had no

luck with their latest ideas of where the Nazi gold might be hidden. Both were ready to leave the island. They were firmly convinced they were wasting their time.

'And the barometer is falling,' said Alexander. 'We can expect some bad weather before long. Even the shoals of fish are veering away from the island. The fishermen say the meltemi is coming.'

'Nonsense,' said the Professor. 'There's not a sign of bad weather. The birds are still flying high.'

'Perhaps so,' said Alexander stubbornly. 'But I bet you one hundred drachmae that by the end of this week, the tides will be up and we have rain.'

'I wouldn't bet on it. You may be right. The storms can come without warning in these waters,' laughed the Professor. 'I'm not going to give you some easy money! Where's that food, I'm hungry.'

Eugenie and Ariadne laid out the

food which Yani had prepared. He had done them proud. There was what Yani proudly called 'Athina-iki mayonéza', cold fish mixed with potatoes, carrots and cucumbers and covered in mayonnaise and sprinkled with herbs. There was also dolmathes, ground minced meat and herbs mixed with rice and rolled tightly in vine leaves, and portions of chicken and salad, with stuffed olives and garlic and peppers as garnish. There were mounds of rather hard rolls and fresh butter and a tasty goat-cheese to follow. And last but not least, a basket of fruit, a strawberry dessert and several bottles of wine, white and red. There was black coffee in flasks and a huge tablecloth. They set everything out neatly and then called the others. All the china and cutlery were neatly packed in a separate basket, and easily set out.

It was a merry meal, Stavros and Petros singing Greek love songs afterwards. The sun came round, strong and brilliant and everyone sought shelter in the mouth of the biggest cave. There it was cool, and for an hour or so, Ariadne slept.

She found the others already awake when she finally roused. The boys were back in the pool, but Alexander and Stephanos were discussing with the Professor the likelihood of exploring these caves. Already they had found they went well back into the mountain side.

Ariadne shivered. She had no great liking for caves and underground passages. She decided to laze and perhaps explore the beach. It was actually the first time she had been right along this particular piece of coast.

The two men decided to go alone. They were both equipped with torches, and as Eugenie felt the same way about caves, Professor Powis decided to stay with her. Why take a day off, and then waste it with other people?

Ariadne watched them walk away together, talking animatedly, and now and then came the unusual sound of his laughter. Yes, she decided, he needed someone of his own, who shared his interests and loved him enough to look after him . . .

She lay on the beach, staring out to sea, and pondered her own future. She would leave Xanos at the very earliest possible moment. There was no future for her, living with her father. She would strike out on her own. If only Michael . . . She sighed and resolutely turned her thoughts from him.

But she was determined to give Eugenie a chance with her father. If she were gone, then her father would surely turn to Eugenie. He already leaned on her, she suspected, even if he was not aware of it. Her absence would give him a push in the right direction! She fought back a tiny twinge of jealousy. She and her father had always been close, but it was right and proper that she should leave the nest and he should start a new life.

Her mind made up, she walked in

the opposite direction to her father and Eugenie. The stony beach was just a narrow strip between sheer cliffs and the choppy blue sea. Here and there, the cliffs appeared to be worn down by countless years of storm water. There were long crevices and gullies, rather like dried up water courses. Now and again she sighted a lone goat staring down at her, a lookout no doubt for a flock hidden farther back behind huge boulders. It was lonely and eerie with only the sound of wheeling birds to disturb the lap of water. She was just about ready to turn back when she saw in the distance a wisp of smoke . . .

Curious, she walked on. She was now more than a mile past the picnic spot. She looked at her watch. She had plenty of time, but she was thirsty, perhaps she could beg a drink from the lonely shepherd, for she supposed the goats she had previously seen belonged to whoever lived in the cottage.

The cottage was farther away than she thought. She must have walked nearly a quarter of a mile before she rounded a corner, and found a stone-built cottage nestled in a crag of rock in front of her. The land around it was sparsely covered with herbage and scrub. She could smell sage and thyme, and drawn up on the rocks below was a boat. So the owners of the cottage were fishermen too.

Several stunted trees grew around the cottage, probably olives and figs. Lemon and orange trees needed more water than they would get hereabouts. A gnarled old vine climbed the landside wall, sheltered from the winds that would blow in from the sea. Water tubs, and several broken-down wheels were the only objects to be seen.

The place looked desolate. The staring empty windows suggested a derelict house, had it not been for the boat which appeared in good condition. Nothing stirred and Ariadne was just going to turn away and go back, when a dog came out of the half-open door to yelp and bark.

The door opened wider and an old woman, nut-brown and wrinkled, came out. Her voluminous black skirt was covered by a white apron, and her grey hair swathed in a black scarf. Her dark eyes were keen however. She frowned at Ariadne.

'What do you want?' She spoke sharply.

'Could I have a drink of water, please?' She was surprised at Ariadne's command of Greek, and looked at her strangely.

She went inside and appeared moments later with a pottery mug filled with crystal-cool water.

'Thank you!' Ariadne smiled her thanks and the old woman drew a sharp breath. She turned into her doorway again. For a full minute she watched Ariadne, and then she said,

'Go away! Go away!' And banged her door.

Ariadne was startled and upset. What had changed the old lady? What had she seen? She sipped her water, and looked

93

around. There was nothing to warrant the old woman's agitation. Slowly she finished the water and carefully placed the mug near the door-step. She turned to go, and saw a youth of about sixteen and a woman who looked like his mother coming along a narrow dirt track, leading a donkey and cart. The cart was laden with driftwood, and a bell tinkled at each movement of the donkey.

She watched them come nearer. The boy had a gay carefree face. He whistled as he walked and he smiled at Ariadne when they came near.

'Good day. Can I help you?' His large white teeth showed in a broad grin. The woman stood back, suspicious and aloof. There was no welcome on her face. Dressed and swathed in black, she was taller and more graceful than the older woman. Her hair was black, streaked with grey.

Ariadne shook her head.

'No.' And went on to thank the boy and explain she had already begged a cup of water and that she was already on her way.

The boy too showed surprise at the ease in which she spoke Greek. He had taken her for an Englishwoman. She laughed and explained she had had a Greek mother. The woman's face changed. She looked hard at Ariadne and then was quickly gone into the cottage.

Her manner puzzled Ariadne. She asked the boy if anything was wrong. He shook his curly head and laughed.

'My mother and grandmother are suspicious of strangers. We see so few people to talk with, and I go mostly alone to Kamari to buy our stores. They like the sea and the wind-swept rocks and the rough pasture for our goats. They do not like the bustle of even a small town like Kamari.' As he spoke, the two women came to stand on the doorstep. The old one looked again at Ariadne and silently nodded her head.

'You must go away from here,' said

the younger, harshly. 'We want nothing to do with your kind. Theodoros! Stop talking and unload the cart and stake out the donkey, that she may eat.'

Theodoros frowned and his eyes flashed.

'I Mamá, you are very rude. Since when do the Kavouras family welcome strangers in this way? I must apologise. My mother is shy but never have I known her like this! I Mamá! Apologise instantly!' The woman's eyes flashed in anger. The old woman disappeared indoors.

'I am not sorry for the way I behave. Not to her! There can be only enmity between us. Go, I say!'

'I Mamá. What do you mean? What words are these?' He left the donkey and came to stand wide-legged in front of his mother.

'Look at her, dolt! Do you not know who she is? She is the daughter of Nina, my sister. Her father is the man who came and took her away, thereby condemning you and us to a life of poverty!' He whirled round and came to stand before Ariadne.

She looked into his eyes, scared and uncertain. Would he carry on the old feud? Astonished, he looked her up and down, and then threw his head back and laughed.

'So you are the daughter of that bad, obstinate Nina. The one who has been said to have gone to the Devil! I have heard many tales about her, and your English father. I never expected to meet the daughter. You *are* Nina Kavouras' daughter, I suppose?' Ariadne nodded, miserably guilty of she knew not what, but very aware of the woman's animosity.

'Then I bid you welcome, cousin, to the Kavouras family.' He held out his hand, and Ariadne grasped it with her Aunt Marigoula looking on. Their eyes met, but there was no welcome in the hot dark eyes.

5

Ariadne entered the cottage with mixed feelings. The two women were openly hostile, and both turned their backs on her. Her grandmother busied herself over a huge cooking-pot over an open fire, and her aunt, stiff-backed, attended to a tray of drying figs in the window, turning them over and over.

Ariadne swallowed a lump in her throat and tried a friendly approach.

'Aunt, what is the matter? Why cannot we be friends?' The woman rounded on her.

'Do not call me Aunt! You are not a Kavouras. Your mother was a traitor to our family! Theodoros is a fool. He has a soft heart because he is young, and all this happened before he was born. We want nothing to do with you!'

Theodoros came to stand beside Ariadne.

'You are wrong, I Mamá, we should learn to forgive and forget past misfortune. This cousin of ours is not to blame for what happened. Nina might not have married a Gavalas, even if she had not met the Englishman.'

'Not married a Gavalas?' His mother's voice rose with astonishment and anger. 'You do not realize what you are saying. She was beautiful . . . the beauty of the family. Of course she would have done. Young Michael loved her.'

'But they quarrelled, remember? And he stayed away from Xanos for years. And Paulo . . . We all know what he is.'

'He may have been different then! Who knows? A girl like Nina might have turned him into a man!'

'I Mamá, you have nursed this resentment in your breast far too long until it has got out of all proportion. I Yayá, what do you think?'

They all turned to Grandmother Kavouras who was standing, wooden spoon in hand, regarding them.

'I lost a daughter for my beliefs.' Her voice was harsh and took on a deep savage note. 'To people like ourselves, what she did was monstrous. She deserted us when we needed her help. This fool of a boy has been brought up soft. If he ever experienced what his grandfather and I went through, he would not talk so! She could have married well, and raised our standing in this community. She did not.'

Ariadne stood up. She bit her lip.

'Then I must go. I am sorry I brought unpleasant memories back again to hurt you. I am very sorry!' The old lady inclined her head. At that moment she looked regal. Ariadne could still see traces of a past beauty.

'I think you mean what you say. But if it will make you feel better, I tell you the memories are here in my heart, for all time. We live and eat with them!'

'I should never have come. Once more I am sorry.'

'It would have been better if we had never met, but I must tell you that had you really been a Kavouras, I should have been proud of you!' There was a smothered exclamation from Marigoula. 'I must say it, daughter . . . I will remember Nina's child with pride.' She turned away to the simmering stew and started stirring again.

'Theodoros, walk with your cousin to where she left her friends and speak with her as you wish, and then say good-bye forever. You cannot be friends. The Kavouras family stand between you and her. Do you understand?'

'Yes, Mother, I understand. I am too young to fight your beliefs now. But some day . . . '

'Some day your Grandmother and I shall both be gone. You then will do as you see fit. Meanwhile . . . we live as we have always lived. Good-bye, daughter of Nina.'

'I am Ariadne . . . I think you should know . . . '

'We do not want to know your name,

so that we do not remember you.' The voice was implacable.

'Then all I can say is good-bye.' She turned to the door.

'Wait.' The tall figure of Marigoula stiffened and she held her head high. For a moment their glances locked. Then she smiled and her face changed. 'We loved Nina, and the more love there is, the more bitterness. I too would have been proud to call you a Kavouras!'

'Thank you.' Somehow, Ariadne felt very humble.

Theodoros was very upset. He had never known his family to be so rude and ungracious! He apologized profusely as they went back along the cliff path. He made excuses for them, and tried his hardest to put things right. Ariadne laughed.

'Theodoros, stop being so melo-dramatic. They were right. I could not expect to come amongst you as if nothing had happened! If only I had stopped to think. But of course

I did not expect to find relatives in that cottage. It was by sheer accident it happened.'

'Then you would not have looked for us?'

Ariadne hesitated.

'I think I should have done, but I was warned that I would perhaps not be welcome.'

'Your father knew?'

'Yes. He said I would be wasting my time. And Michael Gavalas too, warned me.'

'You know him?'

'Yes. It was he who first mentioned the family. My father did not.'

'You knew then about my aunt and Michael Gavalas?'

'Yes. And I do not think they would ever have married. I think it was all a tragic mistake.'

'I do not believe in these family feuds. Will you still remain our friend? Will you and I still remember we are cousins?'

'If you really wish it, Theodoros.

I have no other cousins. It would be nice.'

'Then we shall make a pact. It shall be our secret for now. When I am older we shall meet again and recognize our relationship, I swear.' His eager young face strangely solemn. Then he laughed, showing all his strong white teeth. 'I shall look forward to showing my English cousin off to all my friends! We shall hold a big party and I shall show you how I, and my friends can dance, shoulder to shoulder all night long.'

'I shall look forward to that, Theodoros.'

'And when I marry, my first daughter will be called Ariadne!'

They both laughed, and Ariadne had a warm feeling of belonging. There was a shout ahead. Looking up, Ariadne saw Petros waving.

'Look, my friends have come looking for me. Thank you, Theodoros for walking with me . . . and I shall not forget.'

'Good-bye, cousin Ariadne, we will meet again . . . ' He turned and ran back up the incline. For a moment he stood and turned to her. His hand came up in salute and she waved back, and then he was gone.

She moved slowly towards Petros. How much of this should she tell her father? She decided to say nothing. It would do no good bringing up the past. His future was Eugenie, she was certain.

'Whoever was that?' puffed Petros. 'Stavros and I have hunted and called you for this past hour. Your father and Miss Fafoutis have gone home. We are going with Alexander and Stephanos. They were still exploring their caves when we came looking for you. What have you been up to?' His eyes were curious.

'Just walking. The scenery and the sun cast a spell on me I think. I came across a fisherman's cottage and I stopped to beg a drink. I talked to the family and Theodoros walked me back again. That's all.'

'Come on then. Stavros is just ahead. He's somewhere up that other gully. We were getting worried.'

'I'm sorry, Petros, I did not mean to stay away so long. It just happened.'

They walked on and Petros hallooed for Stavros. He heard him and came to them, not a little cross. He was hot and perspiring, having run up and down several hilly paths looking for her.

'Trust a girl for being unreasonable and expecting us to know what happened to her!' he grumbled.

'I've said I'm sorry, Stavros. I really am. I did not think you would come looking for me.'

'All right, but don't do it again. The next time you might not be so lucky. Going off on your own is not to be recommended around here!'

'Why, whatever do you mean? No one on Xanos would harm me surely?' But unbidden came the face of Paulo, and she felt again the pressure on her neck.

'I'm saying no more,' said Stavros uncomfortably. 'But I have heard rumours. The men gossip in the taverna. They hint, and then clam up, but they do not like their women to walk the hills alone . . . '

'I'll remember, Stavros. I'll not walk alone.' He seemed relieved and said awkwardly.

'They talk a lot of nonsense I think. A full moon cannot have such an influence on a person! A man's mad, or he isn't.'

'And who do they say is mad?' But she knew the answer, before he replied.

'Paulo Gavalas. But I think it is all hooey. He's wealthy and can afford to be eccentric. These people don't understand him, that's all.'

But Ariadne wondered . . . She would dearly have liked to talk to someone about him. What did the villagers know?

Alexander and Stephanos were bathing when they returned. They were excited about the caves, but had found no trace of gold. There were signs of cavedwellers however, and some carvings on the walls put the date at thousands of years ago. They would bring the Professor along one day again, to confirm their findings. They could talk of nothing else.

The next day there was an invitation from Paulo to have dinner with him. He suggested the following night and would be pleased to call and drive them to the Villa Spyros himself. Ariadne replied for herself and her father. They would be delighted to accept. Her father was excited at the thought of seeing the old villa at close quarters.

Ariadne dressed with unusual care the next night. Her heart beat fast at the thought of meeting Michael again. She was so absorbed with thoughts of Michael she did not stop to consider her last meeting with Paulo.

Her dress of daffodil-yellow brought out the lights in her dark hair. It was sleeveless and loose, and flowed rather than hung. She slipped her bare legs into sandals, and caught up an embroidered shawl, for the evenings could become quite cool.

Paulo's eyes lit up when he saw her, and she saw admiration in them. Her greeting was even but rather cool.

'Am I forgiven for my foolish behaviour?' His smile diminished the deed, turned it into a piece of nonsense. Suddenly she was wondering what she had made such a fuss about. Paulo Gavalas was just a very charming man! She relaxed, and gave him her hand.

'Of course. It was nothing. I think Michael made too much fuss . . . '

'Michael is like that. Very melo-dramatic, and serious. Wasted on Xanos, you know.'

The Professor coughed. 'I have often wondered why he stays?'

Paulo smiled wryly.

'I often wonder myself . . . But of course, he is someone here on Xanos, the cousin of Paulo Gavalas, who is the largest landowner on the island.

That counts you know with someone like Michael. Shall we go?'

He drove quickly and well. But for all that, Ariadne was pleased when he drew up outside the Villa Spyros. For one horrible moment, hurtling round a corner there had been an old man astride a donkey . . . It had taken all Paulo's good driving to miss him. For a moment the urbane Paulo changed into a mouthing cursing stranger. And then he was Paulo again, laughing and joking at their near miss.

The villa was a breathtaking poem of architecture. Sprawled in a large garden surrounded by high walls, it commanded a fine view of the sea and coast. The house itself stood above two terraces, and each terrace had overhanging rock plants. A wide stairway connected the two and came up to the front door, which had an outer porch flanked by four pillars in the best Greek temple tradition.

Huge urns stood at intervals on the top terrace, and from there was a superb view of the sea. And yet, Ariadne thought, there was an air of desolation about the place. She could not put her finger on it, but it could look even more wonderful.

Probably it was too ornate, and the white marble walls gave one the feeling of a mausoleum. Her father did not react. The inner hall was tiled in black and white marble, a key pattern bordering the plain square. Each wall held a niche with a half-size statue in it. She recognized Demeter, her delicately carved hand touching an offering of a huge plate laden with fruit, as if preventing a bunch of grapes from falling to the ground. Sheaves of corn behind her threw her into relief. It was as if she blessed all the fruits of the earth. Hermes and Athene were there, but not Apollo.

Professor Powis eagerly went forward to examine and admire. Paulo smiled at his evident pleasure.

'I have many things of interest upstairs, Professor,' he said pointing to the curved marble staircase. 'These are but a few of the poorest. If you would follow me, we shall go to my Exhibition Room. I think you too, Ariadne, will find something of interest.'

They ascended the staircase, which curved upwards on to a balcony. Here too were statues, but now they were of satyrs, and one statue stood out dramatically. It stood on a black basalt plinth . . . a black writhing goddess with a knowing smile. Flames caught in basalt licked around her feet. Surely it was Hecate, the infernal goddess?

Professor Powis stopped before it.

'Now this is very interesting. Hecate was worshipped in an age we know little about. It might indicate the age of this villa. Has she always stood here?'

'As far as I know. This place has not changed since my Grandfather's time. Before that, we have no records. Michael calls it a memorial to the dead. He would like me to give it over to the Greek National Monuments Ministry.

He thinks the place is not healthy to live in.'

'What a shocking idea,' said the Professor. 'There are very few places habitable today with this kind of history. To live in it keeps it in the same condition as when it was first built.' Ariadne did not agree. All very well for a man like her father who lived in the past. He was not aware, or stopped to consider the effect on a man like Paulo. She looked round and shuddered, wondering how Michael could stand living here.

She started. Surely Michael was going to be here tonight? He would make this evening more bearable, although the circumstances of their last meeting were still painful. She broke in on the Professor's ponderous conversation.

'Will Michael be here tonight?' She tried to appear casual and failed. Paulo looked at her and frowned.

'No. You are my guests tonight. Michael is otherwise engaged. Are you disappointed?' Ariadne was disconcerted.

'Oh no. I was just — just wondering . . . '

They moved down a long wide corridor, still tiled in colourful mosaics. This time they gave a wilder, Moorish character. The walls were now white, picked out in gilt. Life-size murals of hunting and drinking scenes faced each other in the upper hall. There were four ornate doorways and Paulo opening one, ushered them inside.

The room was large, light and high-ceilinged. Doors opened out onto a balcony. They were facing inland, away from the sea. This view too was magnificent. The distant mountain olive groves, and in the foreground, a formal garden with a fountain playing.

This room was exclusively a miniature museum. Glass cases and statuary were so placed as to get maximum light. Several gilt chairs were situated so that one could sit and contemplate any object of personal interest. Soon, Professor Powis was oblivious to Paulo and Ariadne. He touched and examined and admired to his heart's content. Urns, bowls, statues of birds and beasts, daggers, a huge bust with half its head missing had him guessing. He was lost in his own world.

Paulo smiled down at Ariadne. Once again his resemblance to Apollo amazed her. Against her will, she felt his fascination.

'You do not want to remain here, amongst all this ancient history? Let us have a drink together next door where we can talk in peace. Professor, your daughter and I are going into the lounge. Will you have a drink sent in here?' The Professor nodded absently. It was doubtful whether he really understood what was said. Ariadne sighed impatiently. Really, her father was the utter limit sometimes!

The lounge faced the same way to the mountain. It was quite a surprise. Too ornate and stately, yet it had an air of comfort. The walls were blue, picked out with raised white scrolls.

The ceiling was a mass of writhing nymphs and chariots, but comfort and indolence was its theme. There were glasses set for pre-dinner drinks on a side table. Two huge divans flanked a huge hearth. Paulo poured Ariadne a glass of golden liquid. She sipped. It was like none she had ever tasted.

'What is it? It is very nice. Not too sweet . . . and refreshing.'

'It is called Bacchanalia's Balm. A recipe long kept secret in the Gavalas family. I shall take a glass for your father to sample.'

He left the room, and Ariadne leaned back on the divan and relaxed. The wine sent a glow to her fingertips and her toes. She felt light-hearted and happy. The world was a good place after all! How on earth had she ever felt suspicious of anyone? There was only good in the world, and the Devil was vanquished!

She seemed to sit quietly and alone for quite a while, drowsy and content. Then she was startled to see him

116

bending over her, smiling and holding out his hand.

'Come, the meal is ready. I talked too long with your father. We shall talk later. Your father wishes to examine some manuscripts after the meal is over.'

Ariadne got unsteadily to her feet. She felt almost drugged! But she put her hand through his arm confidently, and said confidingly,

'You know, I never dreamed this place was so exciting! It is my idea of a perfect home. And you too, are so different to what I expected.'

'Oh, in what way? I am just a very ordinary fellow really.'

'Ordinary?' The thought tickled Ariadne's sense of humour. 'That is the understatement of the year. I would have described you as extraordinary. Do you know there is a strange enchantment about you? A captivating air of magnificent Presence, tinged with a dark nameless something which is all the more fascinating?' Ariadne was

117

astonished at her own awareness. It was like looking through blind eyes that had seen for the first time.

She went into the next room, where a long table that would have seated twenty guests was laid for three at the far end.

A young Greek boy stood waiting to serve. He was dressed in white and wore the traditional Greek pleated skirt. An old woman with piled up white hair and dressed in black stood, with hands folded beside the door. Her face had a disapproving look, and she eyed Ariadne up and down. The Professor who had followed them in, she ignored. She reminded Ariadne of her Aunt Marigoula. Something about her made her want to laugh . . .

Paulo helped her into her chair and the Professor took the other chair. Ariadne noticed he too, looked cheerful and relaxed. Somewhere in her brain, she was aware of a faint warning signal, but the happy feeling persisted and the warning, or feeling was suppressed.

There followed a bewildering number of dishes, after the iced melon soup. Lobster on a bed of hard-boiled eggs and cucumber in a spiced white wine sauce with a snatch of lemon. Moussaká, aubergines with a savoury peppered mince, and grilled souvlakia, veal cubes soused in herb-flavoured oil and grilled over a charcoal brazier as they watched, by the grinning houseboy. And then followed freshwater trout . . . and after that, tiropittakia, small triangles of flaky pastry filled with mashed feta cheese and cooked quickly in boiling oil . . . And with it, a wonderful white wine.

And then when Ariadne felt she could eat no more, there followed a caramel creme, and a cheese-curd tart stuffed with their own fresh-dried raisins and fresh orange peel. And the special Turkish coffee, and with it another glass of Bacchanalia's Balm . . .

Afterwards, the housekeeper took Ariadne away to the bathroom. She motioned to the bathroom door and then opened a door next to it.

'The Master wants you to use this room as your own. Brushes and combs are there for your convenience . . . and anything else you may need.' The dark face was still hostile, and was it her fancy that there was pity in the eyes?

'Thank you, Anyah. May I call you Anyah?'

'I am Kiría Anyah Roussos.' She stood with stiff back and hands folded and staring defiantly at Ariadne.

'Oh! I am sorry. I meant no offence. Thank you, Kiría Roussos.' She smiled timidly at her, and felt a certain self-contempt for feeling intimidated. The woman lowered her eyes and went back along the wide corridor to clear away the dishes.

Paulo was waiting for her in the lounge when she returned. Her father had disappeared, no doubt back to his beloved relics. Paulo indicated the place beside him on the divan.

'Come, sit here and let us get better acquainted. You like my house? It has changed little over the years.'

'Very much . . . It is different. You must be very proud of it. And of the Gavalas name . . . I understand the Gavalas honey and your specially brewed wine is famous throughout Greece. Something to do with the soil and volcanic action, I understand.'

'Something like that. More wine? Some more of the famous Bacchanalia Balm?'

'Oh no! I have already had too much to drink! I feel a little heady now. Thank you very much.'

'Oh, come on. Just another glass will not hurt you. It will make you happy.'

'No, please. I am not used to drinking very much.'

'Then what about a stroll along the terrace? I should like to show you my cactus collection. It is quite impressive.'

'Oh, I did not know you were interested in cactus plants. Are you an expert?'

'I like to think so. We can go through the window here. The cactus-house lies along the terrace.' He looked at her sideways. 'We know so little about each other. I do not even know the colour of your eyes.' Ariadne laughed.

'Does it matter? After all we are just friends. I do not know whether you care for reading, or if you like sailing or swimming. But it does not stop us from being friends!'

'True. But if I like a person, I like to know all there is to know about them. Do you think that unreasonable?'

'No-o, I suppose not.' But she felt uneasy. Paulo could be just a little intense . . .

'Tell me . . . do you remember your mother?'

'A little. But I am afraid her image is getting a little vague. I was only eleven when she died. Why?'

'Do you know you are very like her?'

'I have been told so. Daddy speaks very little of her. You knew her well?'

'I knew her.' Paulo's voice was abrupt. He opened the cactus-house door for them both, and Ariadne proceeded to enter. At once she felt the dry heat, and it put all thoughts of her mother out of her mind.

'Why, how wonderful!' A nearly full moon poured its light through the panes, casting lights and shadows on large and small plants. The shadowed plants appeared bigger and the silvery light made them appear like objects from another planet.

Paulo depressed a switch. Instantly light sprang up, dispersing the weird effect. Now, she could see many of the plants were in bloom. Cream, and all shades of yellow through to orange and red, and in all shapes and sizes. It was a wonderful show.

'And now come and look at my giant fly-trap. A plant I have perfected myself. See, the spines and the size of the fleshy leaves. I consider it one of my best experiments.' They stood beside a huge plant standing by itself.

It had little semblance to the domestic fly-trap that Ariadne had known in England. This plant was monstrous, and seemed to wave a little in the air. As if it was an animal, foraging for food! Ariadne took a step backwards.

'I don't really like it, and it smells of carrion. Not a house-plant I should like to own.' She pulled a face. 'I suppose it is ideal out here. It will keep the other plants free from flies. Was that your intention?'

'Partly. It is also a good way of making sacrifice . . . See, the plant stands on an altar.'

Ariadne saw with amazement that the plant did indeed stand on an altar, and that a statue stood behind.

'To whom is the altar dedicated?' Paulo laughed.

'Can you not guess? Apollo of course! The all omnipotent Apollo. This cactus-house is really a shrine. It is older than this villa. Of a much older civilization. Am I not clever to have utilized it so? Does not all this stir something within you? Is there no hint of an earlier life dormant in your mind?'

Ariadne looked at him with wide eyes. His eyes seemed to grow larger. She felt as if she was drowning in them. For one moment she thought she was rushing through space and into another time.

'Are you not Demeter, come back again? But this time to stay.' She felt Paulo's arms slip about her and his face came down to hers. He seemed to blot out the world, or was it the effects of all the wine she had drunk? The soft velvety voice went on. 'My Demeter, beloved mother of my child! Can we not once again come together? Has the curse of thousands of years ago, been lifted? Surely *this* time all should come right. Did you not love me before you fell over that cliff? Demeter, do not be so cruel again!' She felt his hot breath on her and then the burning kiss, harsh and demanding. There was no love there, just lust and passion, aroused for one purpose only. She struggled, suddenly aware of that purpose.

'No. Leave me alone! I'm not Demeter . . . ' He smothered her words with ungentle kisses, and fumbled at her breast. Her hands somehow reached up to his shoulders and she pushed hard. Hard enough for him to lose his grip of her. He swayed, eyes bloodshot. He looked at the moon, and Ariadne saw the awful anguish on his face, the beautiful god-like face, twisted and evil. She tried to reach the door but failed. Again he held her, and now she tried to scream, but a firm hand over her mouth stopped her.

He carried her to an alcove, bare but for a goatskin rug. He held her tightly but allowed her to sit up.

'Please, I beg of you . . . Let me go to my father . . . '

'Demeter . . . Ariadne . . . you *must* love me! You are the only woman I can find fulfilment with! My own love come back . . . ' He was babbling dementedly and covering her face with frenzied kisses. 'Oh, my love . . . my Love!'

Ariadne felt his onslaught was pushing her deep down into blackness. Gradually his voice came from afar, and there was a thunderous knocking in her brain. Gasping and helpless she fought against oblivion, and then she felt him push her away and she lay with eyes closed on the soft goatskin rug . . . And then an angry voice made her open them quickly again. Michael was staring down at both her and Paulo.

'What in hell's name is going on here?'

Ariadne blushed. Glancing down she saw her skirt was way past her knees. What must he be thinking? She gave a sob. Paulo laughed and pulled out a cigarette and took time to light it. Blowing out smoke into Michael's face he drawled.

'What do you think? A man and a girl together. Use your imagination, man.' Michael stepped back, distaste showing on his face. Ariadne tried to scramble to her feet.

'It's not true, Michael. I came to see his collection of cactus plants. Then he — he — ' Her voice tailed away. Shame at being caught in such an intolerable situation made her turn away. 'Take me back to my father. I want to go home.'

'I can take you back to your father, but you cannot go home. That is why I am home early. There has been a landslide, over the road. I was warned in Xanos about it. Men are even now trying to clear the roadway. It will take all night, and perhaps all tomorrow as well.'

'What! Not the Pericles Boulder?' Paulo swore.

'Yes. I warned you, Paulo, of it, last year and there were signs of a general cracking, more than a month ago. Old Pappadopolous says there was a slight tremor tonight. Just enough to topple the great rock and bring down tons more rubble.'

'Is there anything I can do?' Now

Paulo was all concern. His beloved land was in danger; Ariadne was the least of his concerns.

'No, not a thing. I have already supervised the work, while you were here . . . entertaining Miss Powis!'

With a shock, Ariadne realized he did not really believe her! And he still had no idea just how far Paulo had been prepared to go. She did not like his cool attitude and the formal Miss Powis! Not after . . . She caught her breath at the look in his eyes. Surely he did not think she welcomed Paulo's attentions? A matter of playing one Gavalas cousin against the other?

She turned to go, and found old Anyah standing disapprovingly behind her.

'I will take you to your father, Miss,' she said. 'Master Paulo has been giving her the Bacchanalia Balm,' to Michael. 'He knew I disapproved, but would have his way. Come along, Miss.'

Michael's eyes changed as they watched Ariadne follow Anyah. There was a burning anger within him. He turned to Paulo.

'What right did you have to give a young girl like Ariadne the most powerful aphrodisiac made here? It was monstrous. Do you know what you could have done?'

'I know well enough. I want Ariadne, and I know I could have had her had you not burst in! The Balm did something for me too! I want to father a child! Do you not know what it means to me to feel inadequate? I want to be perfect. Not — ' He suddenly put his head in his hands.

'Bacchanalia Balm will not help you,' said Michael roughly. 'You need medical help. I offered . . . '

'I don't want your offer! With the right woman . . . with Demeter we should have a perfect union!'

'Paulo, I beg of you . . . These illusions are the illusions of a sick man. I promised my uncle to remain with you as long as was necessary. You know that. But proper medical help would cure you and free me. What about it?'

'I am the all-powerful Apollo. Ask Anyah. She knows all. So I do not need your help, or anyone else's. The only person I need is Demeter . . . to give me a son. Nothing else!'

'Well the Balm will not do as you wish. It is for lovers, who really love. All you want Ariadne for, is a body to produce a child. And you too, are incapable. Incapable of loving, and incapable of breeding!' Michael's voice was implacable.

'That's untrue!' screamed Paulo. 'I won't let it be true! I am a God, and Gods are perfect. How dare you say such things?'

'Because the time has come to face facts. You cannot have Ariadne.'

'Why should I not have Ariadne? Who will stop me?'

'I shall. I want Ariadne myself!'

6

Ariadne found her father still absorbed. He had taken copious notes in his note-book and was inclined to be irritable when disturbed. He focussed vacantly on her when she told him what had occurred. Then he took off his glasses, and rubbed his forehead.

'Good Lord! I might not get out to the dig tomorrow! That's a nuisance. I should get in touch with Eugenie, she'll worry about me . . . about us both, I mean . . . ' He had the grace to look hot under the collar. Ariadne hid a smile. Poor Daddy! He was always transparent; too open and honest to hide his feelings!

'Could you not phone the hotel?'

'No good. The line is down.' Michael heard the question as he entered the room. 'The line runs along that road. A couple of poles

132

caught the brunt of the fall.'

'Then we can't get a message through?'

'Not tonight. The meltemi wind is rising, and only the men who are working now will be out there. Everyone else will batten down removable objects and stay behind closed doors. You will have to stay overnight. I hope you don't mind?' He was looking at Ariadne, but her father answered.

'Of course not, Michael. It is good of you to offer. Can I carry on with my examination a little longer?'

'Naturally. Take all the time you need. I myself will show you your room later on.'

The professor turned away and Ariadne looked helplessly at Michael. She looked for some sign that would tell her he had changed his mind. But nothing showed on his face. It had changed too, since she had seen him last. He was thinner and there were new lines grooved from eyes to chin. But the eyes were the same, and it pained her to see the hurt therein.

'Michael!' She put out a hand on impulse. He turned sharply away.

'Don't make it harder, Ariadne. I made a decision, dear. Help me to stick to it!' She saw him tremble.

'If you love me, and I love you, as I really do, who can we hurt? We need have no children. It would be your decision. I love you, Michael. Shall I go down on my knees?'

He turned and swept her into his arms. He kissed her, and for one heavenly moment she felt as if she had come home. Then he buried his head into her neck and groaned.

'Oh, my dear, I do not deserve this. But I could not deprive you of the right to have children.'

'But if it was my decision?'

'Not even then.'

'But why?'

'Because the time might come when our love wasn't enough. You might yearn for children and blame me. Then, the delicate feeling between us would be destroyed. We should be left with nothing.'

'Michael, I swear I should never worry about a family. I understand your fear. Oh darling, could we not try?' She clung to him, sobbing. He stroked her hair, his dark face a greyish-white.

'My darling. You do not know what you are asking. There is more to it than that. There is a history of violence . . . The Gavalas twins were both tainted. Do you know they tried at different times to kill each other? I couldn't bear you to run the risk.' They clung together.

Old Anyah stood outside, her face agonized. She had seen all that was going on. She had not understood all, because they had been speaking in English, but she knew enough to know what it was all about. Her thoughts whirled. It was good that Michael should have this girl. It was Paulo she loved and dreaded seeing with a woman. Her disapproval of Ariadne

135

disappeared. If she loved Michael, she should have him . . . But a gasp behind her made her look round. Paulo stood, eyes distended and a vein pulsing at his temple. He pushed Anyah aside like a rag-doll.

'What is all this talk of rejection, Michael? You don't want to marry her?' Both Ariadne and Michael turned to see him in the doorway, Anyah just behind. Michael kept his arm about Ariadne. 'Well? What do you mean, Michael? Only half-an-hour ago you told me I couldn't have her, you wanted her yourself!' Michael drew a deep breath.

'Paulo! I warned you . . . '

'Go on, tell her! Make it clear. You don't want to marry her, but you want her! Now I, I really want to marry you,' turning to Ariadne. 'Can you beat that? My good prissy cousin wants a mistress . . . ' Ariadne looked up at Michael, shocked and wide-eyed. She pulled away from him, uncertain. She backed away and turning with a sob, ran out of the room. Anyah followed, clucking sympathetically. All she could understand was that matters were not right between this girl and Michael, and that Paulo had been making mischief . . .

Anyah stayed with Ariadne until she was settled in bed. She kept muttering about poor Michael and poor Paulo, and at one point cried into her apron. How she loved Paulo and would do anything for him, but that Michael was good too. She had to do right by both. God above knew how her loyalties had been torn! Ariadne tried to give words of comfort, but when she wanted it most, her Greek failed her.

But she was filled with curiosity. For the moment it dimmed her own unhappiness. It was as if she had grown a tough crust around herself to shield her from pain. She could not bear to think of Michael. Someone else's pain was easier to cope with. And Anyah certainly was suffering.

The old woman's stiff back had

crumpled. She now looked ten years older, and her cheeks seemed to have dropped in. But it was the look in the eyes which shocked Ariadne. They were haunted and frightened. She came to stand beside the bed when Ariadne was settled down.

'Is there anything else I can do for you Miss? Anything else you want?'

'No, Kiría Roussos. You have been very kind. I only wish I could do something for you . . . '

'It would help me if you and Master Michael . . . He needs someone. He has the great responsibility here. No one knows better than I. I do not know you well, but I think you could be the one.'

'I thought that too,' said Ariadne sadly, 'but now, I do not know what to think.'

'I do not know what you have in mind, but Michael is a good boy, and — well — not as Paulo. Paulo must not marry. I love him as a mother, and God forgive me for my words, *but he must not marry*!'

'But why not? Why do you insist that he cannot, and Michael can? Are they not of the same blood? Do you know something?' Ariadne sat up in bed, suddenly alert. Was there some mystery about the cousins. She tried to remember what she had heard about Anyah. She had mothered Paulo when his mother died. Michael too had come in for some mothering. As a small boy he had visited the Villa Spyros fairly frequently until the feud had started between the twin brothers. She wondered what it had all been about.

Anyah tightened her lips, and did not answer. She moved to the door and then turned.

'I have said too much now. It is not fitting to talk of the past, and the dead who go with it!' She closed the door quietly behind her, leaving a very puzzled Ariadne to toss and turn in the strange bed. Anyah's words repeating themselves hourly in her head . . .

But it was not only Anyah who kept

Ariadne awake. Now, in the quiet of the night, memories of Michael came back. A loving despairing Michael, who was more real to her than the Michael conjured up by Paulo. Which was the real Michael? And as she lay alternately weeping and agonizing, the wind rose and the casements rattled. She now understood the concern when the islanders warned that the meltemi wind was coming.

And there was something else. Surely the bedposts had rattled? And was that the tinkle of glass against glass. Not an earth tremor as well as this awful wind? She sat up, hugging the sheets around her, not knowing what she should do. But it did not happen again so she put it down to the wind and a highly fraught imagination.

The next morning found her heavy-eyed and suffering from a headache. Anyah took one look at her and ordered her to lie still. She brought good strong coffee and fresh rolls and butter and delicious fig and lemon conserve. She

140

also brought aspirin and stood over her while she took the dose.

She felt cared for and cosseted, and in her heart was ashamed of her first impressions of Anyah. Now she was much calmer and told Ariadne that Master Michael and her father had breakfasted much earlier and gone down to help with the clearing of the road. Of Paulo she never said a word, and Ariadne did not like to ask.

By lunch-time she felt a new person. She bathed and then found that Anyah had washed out her underwear and it was dried and aired. Ariadne tried to thank her, but Anyah waved her thanks aside.

'It is nothing. I would do more for Master Michael's lady. My greatest wish is for him to marry. It hurts me to see him buried in this place. I would that he was free. But I too know that he made a promise to Paulo's father, and a promise must be kept when honour is at stake. But if he would marry you, then perhaps the burden would not appear so great.'

'You don't understand, Kiría Roussos. He will not marry me because the Gavalas blood is tainted. We love each other, or at least I love him . . . '

'And he loves you, never fear. I have watched his eyes. But tell me again why he will not marry you.'

'He says his father and Paulo's father were both mad, or at least had violent tendencies. And being twins made it all so much worse. Oh, Kiría Roussos, I am so miserable!' She broke down and sobbed on the old woman's shoulder.

'There, there. Nothing is as bad as it seems. But call me Anyah. I feel we understand one another now. I am sorry I was unfriendly at first. Put it down to an old woman's fear of Master Paulo wanting to marry. I thought it was he who wanted to marry you.'

'He does. Did you not know? Last night they quarrelled over me. Paulo attacked me and called me Demeter. He is mad. There is no question about it. He suffers from delusions and believes himself to be a reincarnated Apollo. He is obsessed with the thought of fathering a son. And Michael has the same blood in his veins. Now do you see? He is frightened to marry me.'

'Oh dear God! Not again. We must not go through all that again! I would rather see him dead than that should happen!'

'What are you talking about? You are frightening me.'

The old woman shuddered.

'I thought Paulo was getting over his delusions. For the last few years he has lived quietly and busied himself in his plans for his big hotel. Now that he has seen you, all the old beliefs are back. It was all partly my fault. He was a lovely boy and I encouraged him to believe in re-incarnation. It was done in the first place so that he would read our own history. He was proud of our island history, and especially that of the Gavalas family.'

'Did he never show any signs of disturbance?'

'Not at first. He was lonely and sensitive. He looked forward to his young cousin coming to stay, and they roamed the hills and explored the beach together. He was at his best then, and the young Michael adored him.'

'But what happened? What made him change?'

'When he was seventeen, he fell in love with a village girl. She was a little older than he and I remember him coming home crying. She had laughed at him and called him half a man. That night he changed. He built a wall around himself. His world became a fantasy world where he was God and the only dominant person in it. When Michael came again to stay, he was not wanted. Paulo had no time for him.'

'And what about my mother?'

'Ah, she brought everything to a head. Michael fell in love with her when he was about seventeen. She was a little older. They fooled around for a whole summer, and Paulo did not seem to care. But she was a lively girl and Michael did not like her eyeing the other boys and they quarrelled. Michael went away.'

'And then my father came to work on the island.'

'And all the girls were after him. They all wanted the good-looking Englishman, and I think your mother took up the challenge and encouraged him. He fell in love with her and they married.'

'Mother loved Daddy. They were happy together!'

'Perhaps. I do not really know, but she still had a roving eye. I *do* know that Paulo became fascinated with her. And about the same time it was said he wandered the hills when the moon was full, beseeching Zeus, his Heavenly Father to send him a sign that he was indeed Apollo. And if he was Apollo, to send him his mate, Demeter.'

'And was my mother the sign he wanted? Was she his Demeter?'

'He liked to think so, but for Nina

Kavouras, he was only a diversion, someone to be laughed at . . . and she laughed!'

'Then — then my mother was pushed over that cliff?'

'No. I do not think so . . . Paulo came back that night, convinced that Demeter had escaped him. He was in an excitable state and his father and I restrained him and kept him sedated until long after the inquest.'

'It was said that Paulo seemed to be in another world.'

'Yes. Whether his father was right or not, we kept him quiet. And it was then his father first thought of Michael coming back to Xanos to watch over him. I welcomed it because . . . ' She stopped suddenly and turned away. 'Will you have lunch now? I shouldn't chatter so much.'

'Anyah, what is it you know and we don't?' They stared at each other and Anyah dropped her eyes.

'Have you ever seen a picture of the Gavalas twins?' Ariadne shook her head. Anyah gave a great sigh. 'Come with me, I will show you something.'

Ariadne followed the old woman down to the house-keeper's room. She silently pointed to an oil-painting hung over the wide mantel-piece. It was of two boys of about ten years. Their arms were entwined and at first glance they were identical twins.

Ariadne studied them both. The more she studied the more she could see the subtle differences. One of the boys had a broader face than the other. They both had incredibly fair hair and tawny eyes . . . But one had a fuller mouth and the other's nose seemed a little tiptilted, but so minute were the differences they would not be noticed unless, like Ariadne, they were looking for something . . .

'Which one is Michael's father?'

'The one on the left.' Anyah sounded peculiar. Ariadne glanced sharply at her, and then something clicked in her mind.

'Michael does not resemble him. I wonder why?'

'Because his wife was already with child when she married him!' The voice grated harshly, stopping Ariadne in her tracks. 'You know what this means?'

'Yes,' whispered Ariadne. 'Michael is not a Gavalas!'

7

During her lunch, Ariadne could think of nothing else. She wanted to run down the road to find Michael and tell him that he was not a Gavalas. That he was . . . what? Her deep feeling of heady exhilaration evaporated. How would he take the news? He would feel a certain relief . . . overwhelmingly so, that no madness, even only slightly, was in his veins. But he was proud too of being a Gavalas . . . She faced a dilemma.

But it was a dilemma she was not yet to combat. One of the young Greek villagers came up to the villa in an old fish-cart and told her he had orders to take her back to Xanos. They had cleared half the road and the cart could ease its way past. She said good-bye to Anyah, who lent her a voluminous black shawl to wrap herself up against the wind. She clung to her for a moment. The old woman said little, but as the cart moved away, ran after it and shouted,

'Remember now, make him understand. His mother was a good woman . . . ' The rest was whipped away on the wind. Now, as the cart creaked and jostled over the rough road, she wondered if it was possible . . . Or would pride turn him away from her . . . There was hurt for him either way.

The youth whistled as he drove. Apart from the usual pleasantries he was silent. But as they approached the narrow gap in the roadway, he spoke.

'Master Paulo has been working all night. He has the strength of ten men. He blames himself for the fall. Something to do with the old altar stone — the Pericles Boulder. One marvels in the strength of the man, because he is quite old.'

'Not that old!' laughed Ariadne. 'He is just in his prime.'

'My mother says he was wild, when she was a girl, and she is over forty.'

'It only seems old to you. How old are you?'

'Nineteen. And I am married with a small son.' He laughed and flashed his teeth. 'Are you surprised?'

'Very. You are young to be married.'

'Not so. My parents married young. I grew up with Katya, and it was considered good business for the two families to be joined in matrimony. Two families can work and share, better than one.'

'But you love Katya?' The boy hesitated and looked a little puzzled.

'I'm fond of Katya. I suppose I do love her. We work well together and we do not quarrel, unless I stay at the taverna too long. Then she is a virago . . . I think I am a lucky man.'

'If you know you are lucky, then you must love her!' Ariadne smiled at him. 'But what difference does it make to your family?'

'We share a boat, and we fish.

Katya's father and two brothers work with me and my father and my two brothers. We share everything. Soon, my sister marries, and her husband's family will share. We shall buy a bigger boat and do some real fishing, and then we shall be able to sell our catches to the fish factory.'

Ariadne nodded absently. So that was why Nina's family had been against the English marriage! There had been no joining of families and therefore no prosperity. Poor Nina! No wonder they had called her traitor.

Passing the landslide was quite frightening. Rock was still sliding and falling at intervals. She saw Michael and her father, dirty and nearly unrecognizable, and waved as the cart jerked its way past. Of Paulo there was no sign.

She found the camp in a state of flux when she arrived. Eugenie was already there with Petros and Stavros. Some of the diggings had caved in. The Professor had contrived to send a message to Eugenie, and typically of her father, it was more to do with the site than Eugenie herself.

She grinned wryly, and showed Ariadne the message. Apart from telling her they were safe, and the word love at the end, it could have been a message from a boss to any secretary in the world! Ariadne handed it back and said,

'A good job you understand him, Eugenie. I know how you feel for each other. It sticks out a mile, but you will have to educate him, I fear.'

'I'd not have him any different. I love him as he is. Do you mind?'

'Not in the least. It is time I made a new life for myself. I mean to strike out on my own when this job is done.'

'There is no need . . . Your father and I have talked things over. We want you with us.'

'Then it is all settled?'

Eugenie nodded and beamed. 'And we really do want you with us.'

'Thank you. It is nice to know I

shall always be welcome, but, as I say, I should like a life of my own.' They smiled at each other. It was like two mothers disposing of a baby, and both were satisfied.

She found Elias Haralambos supervising the saving of the dig. The wind had done considerable damage and certain shoring up posts had collapsed which meant careful digging so as not to damage anything not yet found under the surface.

He was a jumping mass of nerves. He fairly trembled while the boys picked their way through the rubble. He turned a harrassed eye on Ariadne.

'Where is the Professor? He should be here. I can't be held responsible for any damage these men cause.' He eyed her owlishly through his glasses. 'Is anything wrong?'

'There has been a landslide on the coast road. Dad is helping to move the earth. He sent a message to Eugenie. He will be along later.'

'He should have sent me a message.

After all, I am second in command. It is disgraceful the way I am treated! All this responsibility! I am an archaeologist, not a common labourer.'

'Oh, Elias, no one said you were! You are managing beautifully and after all it is an emergency.'

'Well, I suppose I can cope, but it's not doing me any good, all this strain. I have a nervous head you know. I really must take things easier.'

'I'm sure you must. I can see you have done well. I shall tell my father so . . .'

'You think so?' His face brightened a little. 'I take things too seriously. That's my trouble. I think I'll just go and take a pill and then I'll be able to carry on a little longer.'

'I'm sure you will. I don't know where you find the strength, but being an expert, I know you will want to watch developments. This slight lull in the wind is only temporary, you know. We can expect it rough again later.'

'Well it's no good standing talking

to you. I must get on. The Professor will be relying on me.' He fussed away, and Ariadne smiling, watched him go, newly heartened and full of his own importance.

Stephanos and Alexander, not interested in the site, were poring over maps. They looked up at her entrance in the makeshift office. Both looked weary, and as if they had just had a difference of opinion. Stephanos said sourly,

'I've just been saying to Alexander here, that there's no gold on these islands. I think it has been recovered, and is probably in a Swiss bank. We're chasing rainbows. I vote we go home.' Alexander shook his head.

'He can do what he likes. I'm staying on. I've had an idea.' Stephanos laughed derisively.

'He's got a mad idea of exploring Demeter Island. He's not convinced that it's not been visited for years. He's got this odd theory . . . '

'Damn it, man, it's a good theory!'

'What is it, Alexander?' Ariadne was

suddenly curious. She too had felt an urge to visit that strange holy place.

'Well, no one can land a boat on it, right? You can sail all round it and there are nothing but sheer cliffs, except for one place!' Ariadne looked inquiringly from one to the other. Alexander went on,

'Those sheer cliffs drop suddenly to a kind of plateau, still too high for a boat to land . . . But during a high tide and when the meltemi wind blows, that is another matter!'

'You mean it could be possible? But it could be dangerous! There are hidden rocks. The boat would never survive in that wind!'

'The Greek caiques are shallow-built for that reason. I think it could be done. Stephanos says not.'

'I think he's mad. I'll not hear of it.'

'Frightened, Stephanos? I think it worth a try. Takis Pappadopolous is willing to go. He's a good boatman and knows the currents. We can wait until high-tide and have one stab at it, surely. Come on, what do you say?'

'Well, I'm not frightened, whatever you think. I just think we're wasting our time and sweat. But if you are determined . . . '

'Good lad. If we find nothing, I promise that's the finish. We'll go back and report nothing doing.'

'If we ever get back!'

Ariadne was worried. It seemed a mad plan, but she took heart when she knew Takis Pappadopolous was to be with them. If anyone could steer a boat onto that island he would be that man. She wished her father was there, or Michael. There was not much she could do in these circumstances, so she went back to Eugenie.

Eugenie was surprisingly casual about the whole affair.

'They know what they're up against. Stop worrying! Here, if you want something to do, help me. Pack those specimens with cotton-wool and tabulate them; the small objects go into the chests with small drawers. The larger stuff in individual cases. It would be a help. I'm getting a little behind.' So for a while they worked companionably together. It gave no time to think about Michael and the problem confronting her.

Then in the late afternoon her father returned. Most of the work had been finished. The road was now open. He looked tired and grey. Ariadne left Eugenie to fuss over him. She still had to decide about telling Michael about his parentage. Was she justified? Had Paulo sown a seed of doubt within her? She felt unsure of him and of herself.

She walked for some time alone. She must get away from everyone and fight this battle herself. For a while she walked along the beach until she was under the cliff where her mother had fallen. There was a narrow path winding upwards from the beach to the plateau above. She decided to climb. The exercise might blow away some of the cobwebs.

Panting and clawing, she scrambled and clung, until she reached the top. For awhile she lay on a sunwarmed rock, too overcome to admire the view . . . Then, recovering somewhat she examined the little plateau. It was really a niche in the rocks, with the narrow path continuing to the very top and coming out near the lemon and orange groves belonging to the Hermes Hotel.

All around in the rock crevices were tufty stubborn plants, clinging for life with deep roots and throwing out coral flowers. There were ragworts and saxifrages, and a form of bird's eye. It was a natural lovers' trysting-place.

All at once she needed her mother. Her heart reached out for her. This was a time when she needed a mother's guidance. She put her head down on the smooth rock and cried. Somehow, everything seemed so unfair.

The storm of tears passed. And she was aware of the wind rising again, and a patter of rain in that wind. It was darker, and she sat up alarmed. From where she was, she could see the choppy waves as if churned by a mighty hand. The sea lost its bright azure hue and appeared grey. White flecks of foam indicated the rocks underneath. Uneasily she thought of Stephanos and Alexander. Had they started out on their mad quest?

There was a sound behind her. She looked round and saw a slithering shape. The man was bent nearly double, his head away from the wind. He was half-way down the cliff and coming towards her. As she watched he raised himself and waved, his voice lost on the wind. It was Paulo.

Everything in her shrank away from him. What was this madman doing here? She looked uneasily round, but no one else was in sight. Stumbling and sliding he reached the flat surface and walked over to her. His appearance was peculiar. She noticed that he was unchanged and unwashed from the night before, and his chin needed a razor. At this moment the likeness to Apollo was blurred. But it was his expression that frightened her. Exultation had him in its grip. The wind, fierce and threatening, whipped his senses to a high pitch.

Now, he smiled and came to her. His arm went about her, and he laughed and waved his arm to the sea.

'Now what do you think of my domain? This untamed land and sea. I prayed for a sign. I am right. It is time for Apollo to come into his own. And I called you and you came. Does not that prove something to you?'

'What do you mean? You did not call me.'

'Silly child. Not literally of course. But I called. And you are here to prove it. Do you not know what this place means to me? Of course you do! You used to meet me here. You loved me then. I was a fool. I should have taken you. You offered so much. It could have saved so much heartache. But it was I who doubted then. Me, the great

Apollo, doubting my own manhood! You were willing, but you laughed at my doubts and called me callow youth . . . It will not happen again!'

'But you are mistaken. I am Nina's daughter. Remember?'

'You are the one who makes mistakes. She was Demeter, and escaped me by falling over the cliff. She laughed at me, and I rushed at her in fury. She stepped back . . . But you remember! You are Demeter, reincarnated. Sent by Zeus to give me a second chance! I beg of you, this time . . . ' He pulled her into his arms and Ariadne was aware of a sharp sweet smell on his breath. The pungent smell of that never to be forgotten Bacchanalia Balm! As his face came down to hers she noted the glazed look in his eyes. It was as if he was under the influence of drugs!

She fought him off, but not before he had smothered her with kisses. They swayed together on the edge of the cliff, and for one hideous moment, Ariadne thought they would both go over. Then inspiration came to her. She shouted.

'Look at the sea! It is rising fast. The whole of the harbour is in danger!' It was true. The waves even now, were flinging themselves over the jetty below.

Paulo slackened his hold, his mind temporarily diverted. Ariadne took advantage and quickly slipped out of reach.

'And see Demeter Island. It is in danger of being swamped.' She leaned against the rocks, spent. For a moment it was as if her mother reached out to her.

Then Paulo gave a great cry, which jerked Ariadne into awareness. He pointed to the little island in the bay.

'That boat! What is it doing there? Do you know anything about this?' He grabbed Ariadne by the hair and faced her to the sea.

'By the Gods, if I thought you did, I would throw you over this cliff, as you went before!' He spoke through clenched teeth. A stream of obscenities came from him. And then, 'The shrine! Whoever it is must not put hands on the shrine! It would be sacrilege. You — you — damn you, Demeter, is this another diversion to enable you to escape from me?' He struck her on the side of the head and she felt herself lost in a dark void.

Heavy rain on her face brought her round. She lay, still half-stunned, wondering what she was doing there. She was alone and the rain was leaping off the ground in icy splinters. Her clothes were sodden and her long wet hair blew in her face. She had never been so cold. She felt drowsy and could have dozed but something in the back of her mind nagged her to start moving.

She staggered to her feet, and the fitful moon, barely discernible behind fast scudding clouds reminded her of the storm. It was now dark, with the darkness of barely reflected moon on water. She wondered about Paulo. Where had he gone? There was something about a shrine. She felt her way to the narrow cliff path going upwards. It was slippy and near-impossible to climb.

She sobbed, the pain in her head a merciless throb. Then followed a scramble for life. The wind tore at her hair. Her stiff and cold limbs refused to do her bidding. She grew angry with herself. This was no way for an islander's daughter to behave! It was as if her mother chided her and spurred her on!

Clawing and feeling for a griphold, she felt her way upward. Twice she slipped backwards and had to try again. Each step was painful and she felt wet sticky blood where she grazed her knees and shins on spurs of rock.

But she won in the end. It seemed hours before she lay on the ground up above the rocks at the mercy of the full force of the wind. For a while the whole world was just that little spot where she lay. But the heat and sweat generated from the desperate

166

scrambling subsided, and again she shivered. She must move.

But now it was easier. She could not stand because of the gale force wind, so she crawled in the direction of the citrus groves. There, more sheltered, even though the wind whipped the branches of the trees nearly to the ground, she was able to stand.

Then a hard bump on the head warned her of falling fruit. So, doubling up to protect herself, she half-ran, half-staggered towards the Hermes Hotel.

There was a light in the small house that housed the laboratory, before the hotel. A wild hope made her hammer on the door.

Michael, startled, caught the staggering figure as she slumped against the door. Quickly he carried her indoors, kicking the door shut with his foot. He laid her gently on to the couch. She opened her eyes as he fumbled with her dress.

'My God, what have you been doing? I thought you were with your father and Eugenie.'

'I — I — I was out walking, and I climbed to the little plateau overlooking the village . . . Paulo came . . . Oh, Michael, it was awful!' She buried her head in his arms, and shuddered. Michael smoothed the wet hair back from her face.

'There now, you're safe. We must get you out of these wet things, or you will catch pneumonia.' He got up to find her something to wear. She pulled at his hand.

'Don't leave me, Michael. I can't bear to be left . . . '

'Dearest, I'm just going into the bedroom. I'm going to find you some pyjamas. You must change.'

'What is this place? I thought you only had a laboratory here.'

'It is a chalet, or what you would call a self-contained unit. Paulo and I both use it. He, if he is late in town and I, if I have been working late. It is a useful private place.'

'And Paulo hasn't been here tonight?'

'No. Why should he be? But wait,

and tell me when I get you the pyjamas.'

Ariadne shivered, not just because she was wet. Michael returned with some gay silk pyjamas in pale green. He also brought a bowl of water to bathe her legs, and plasters, and then busied himself making coffee while she changed. He arrived back from the little kitchen just as she sank wearily into the cushions on the couch. Her whole body felt as if she had been beaten.

There was a good lacing of Scotch whisky in the coffee and Ariadne drank it gratefully. It caused a warm glow to permeate her whole body. She felt her cheeks burn, and knew the spirit was having effect. As he fixed the plasters, he said,

'Now tell me why Paulo may have called.'

'I was on the plateau when Paulo saw me and climbed down the little path. He had been drinking that special wine . . . '

'My God, not the Bacchanalia Balm?'

'Yes, I'm sure it was the Balm. It has a peculiar smell . . . '

'Lethal to a man suffering from delusions. Usually he doesn't care for the taste. He must be in quite a state. Did he — er — er . . . pester you?'

'He thought I was Demeter, and insisted that I was my mother, come back to give him another chance.'

'Oh God, was he violent? Did he try to harm you? I must know, Ariadne. I have a decision to make, and you know what it is.'

'Oh Michael, you couldn't lock him away! Not Paulo. He loves the hills and the sea. To shut him away would surely send him quite mad, and people would say you only did it to control the Gavalas fortune!'

'You would never think that?'

She shook her head. 'But where is he now? To get away from him I pointed out that Demeter Island was in danger of disappearing under the waves. He looked out to sea and saw a boat trying to land. It was then he hit me. He seemed beside himself. I fell and knocked myself out. He was gone when I came to.'

'Darling, what you have suffered, and how frightened you must have been! Now I want to tuck you up in bed, and go and look for him. My car is outside, I'll go home first and see if he is at the villa.'

'Don't leave me, Michael! Not tonight. I'm being a weak fool, but not after . . . '

'I'll take you to Eugenie. She will look after you.' He looked worried. He took her hand and felt her pulse, but was satisfied it was only reaction.

'No, I would rather go with you. Please take me, Michael. Please . . . '

He could not bear the look in her eyes. He weakened.

'You can stay with Anyah. I can leave a message for your father. Will that do?'

'Anything is better than being left alone to wonder what is happening.'

'All right. Now move quickly. I'll find you some trousers and a jersey. You can slip them over those pyjamas. You will have to wear your own shoes, but I've got some fine socks you can wear. And here's my fishing-jacket. It will keep out the wind, and there is a hood. So you should be warm enough. Can you walk?'

She stood up on strangely weakened legs. It was an effort, but she managed to hide the trembling. She rolled up the trouser legs to make them fit and looked like a rag-doll. Michael gave her a look and laughed. He hugged her, kissing the top of her head.

'There's not a lot of you, but what there is, is all grit. I only wish . . . ' His voice tailed off. She knew what he was going to say, and it reminded her of something.

'Michael, I have something to tell you . . . I just found out today . . . '

'Darling, leave it for now. We've not a lot of time. Tell me tomorrow . . . I wonder who was mad enough to put a boat out in this weather?'

'It was Takis Pappadopolous, and Stephanos and Alexander. Alexander had some mad notion of landing on the island, and looking for that gold.'

'Of all the mad hare-brained plans! I wonder Takis offered to take them. He knows what a risk he would be taking!'

'But that was the whole point. Alexander had this idea of being able to land a boat at high tide during the meltemi, when the tide would be unusually high. I told Paulo, and he went berserk. He talked of a shrine. As if he had been there before!'

'A shrine you say? I wonder . . . Come on, I don't think we have any time to lose!'

He let them both out of the house and into the gale-force wind. Ariadne gasped, and felt her courage failing her. But Michael grasped her to him and putting his arm about her, ran for the car. He had the car's engine ticking over in an instant.

Then in blinding rain and wind they started their hazardous journey. It took them twice as long as usual to reach the villa, and when they got there, found it shuttered and barred against the elements.

'Good old Anyah. Trust her to see to the house. This villa is her life. Nothing must harm that!'

He hammered on the door. For a while Ariadne thought the place was deserted. Michael swore. The rain was running in rivulets down their faces and Ariadne felt as wet as she did before. But at last, the bolts were drawn and Anyah looked fearfully out.

'You've taken your time! You look frightened. Is anything the matter?' Michael helped Anyah to shut the door, and she slipped the first bolt into place as he held the door. Then she burst into tears.

'It's Paulo! He came here raving like a madman about two hours ago. I couldn't understand what it was all about, but he was shouting about the shrine being defiled, and a lot of rubbish about Demeter and the island. Surely no one can get onto the island? Oh my poor Paulo! I think at last his mind has gone. It is a judgment!' She rocked herself and then buried her head in her apron. 'My baby, my little Paulo, cursed since the day I gave you birth!' she moaned, oblivious to her small audience.

'What do you mean, woman, about Paulo being your baby?' Michael shook her and the sobs subsided.

'I was your Uncle's mistress and gave him a son a month before his wife was delivered of a stillborn child. He made her accept my child in his place, and the shock of knowing about his mistress killed her. She had no desire to live and just wasted away. Before she died, she cursed him and Paulo, and told me I should see an end to the sin and my heart would be broken. And it is true!'

'But I thought my father and Uncle

quarrelled over who should marry her. I thought my Uncle loved his wife . . . '

'They quarrelled over me! It was I who first came between them! I separated the twin brothers who had always been all in all to each other. I was to blame and I'm paying now. Do you know what it has been like to watch Paulo during his evil moods? I live in fear and terror of the full moon.' Her voice sank to a whisper. 'It is then I fear . . . murder. Paulo is quite capable of it!'

Michael looked stunned, and then he put out a kind hand.

'Who can judge another? You must have loved my uncle very much to deceive his wife so.'

'Love? I worshipped him! He was all man. A man any woman would follow to the ends of the earth. His wife was . . . faugh! A poor snivelling creature at the best. Not worth the husband she got. I was proud that my son was recognized as a true Gavalas. I am paying now!' She turned away.

'Where is he now? Where is Paulo?'
'He talked of the shrine to Demeter. He was as one possessed. He struck me when I tried to prevent him going. He's gone to the island of Demeter!'

8

'Demeter? But how? One man couldn't manage a boat in this weather! Anyah, do you know?'

'I don't know. But I *do* know that he goes there! Once or twice he has disappeared when you have been away in Xanos. I have looked for him and he has been nowhere in the grounds. I have searched every inch!'

'Why have you never told me?'

'Because he threatened me! I asked him once where he had come from. I had looked everywhere for him and then I suddenly found him on the terrace, dirty and cobwebby. I couldn't understand it, and he was angry, so angry.'

'Hm, whereabouts on the terrace, was he?'

'Near the arbour ... Well, just outside his cactus-house. He spends

178

a lot of time there . . . '

'That's it! Could there be some kind of underground passage? But it's impossible. How could there be?'

Ariadne frowned, and thought hard.

'Paulo said the cactus-house was a small temple. He described it as a lodge.'

'Of course! A lodge-keeper guards the gateway to the big house! We used to play in the little temple as children. There is an ancient statue of Apollo there . . . Paulo was proud of it. Even in those days I remember his strange absorption in the history of the Gods. I think we should take a look.'

'Michael, if you find Paulo, you'll not hurt him?' Anyah's eyes reflected her love and worry.

'Anyah, my dear, I should never hurt Paulo. He was as a brother to me. Believe me, I only want to help him. Trust me.'

Anyah looked long at him and then clasping his hand, brought it up to her mouth, and kissed it.

'You've always been a good boy, Michael. I do trust you.'

'Good. Then look after Ariadne for me, and make her rest. She had a bad time tonight. And rest yourself.'

'Michael, I couldn't rest easy, knowing you were searching alone for Paulo. I must help.'

'Darling, you look all in.'

'I am tougher than you think. Let me look with you for the opening of this secret passage . . . if it exists.'

'Come along then, it must be in the temple, if anywhere. Anyah, if we let ourselves out onto the terrace, can you bolt the doors again if I hold them together?' She nodded. He turned to Ariadne. 'Now you are sure? You are damp again, and probably will get wetter. You still want to come?'

'Yes, yes, Michael. I would much rather be with you, than imagine the worst . . . and not know.'

'Then, Anyah, be ready to slam the bolts.' He opened one of the double doors and immediately the wind blew the curtains and an ornament nearby shattered on the floor. They both slipped out and Michael put his shoulder to the door to hold it. There was the sound of bolts sliding into place and they turned to face the wind.

Ariadne had the sensation of choking. The wind caught her throat and Michael had to drag her along to the little temple. Once inside, they stood holding each other and regaining their breath. Michael smiled down at her.

'All right? Just tell me if you change your mind. You can always go back.'

'No, carry on. I am worried about Paulo too. I have a terrible feeling . . . '

They searched the small room. The temple consisted of an inner sanctum, which could be described as an alcove. It held the statue of Apollo, and the altar stone bearing the huge fly-trap plant. The whole thing was raised up on a dais, with three steps running all round it. There was a carved archway in white marble separating this inner place to the temple proper. There was room for several people to kneel and pray. Marble pillars held up the ornate roof, and openings for glassless windows had been altered, to accommodate modern frames.

Where once had been marble window-seats, there were now rows and rows of cacti in all sizes and shapes. Many were in flower and some had a sickly rotten smell.

They looked around, behind and under the staging for the cactus-plants, and Michael particularly examined the square paving-stones. There was no sign of recent disturbance. Michael looked at the inner sanctum walls, especially that directly behind the statue. Everything seemed solid.

'There *must* be an opening here!' fretted Ariadne.

'If there is, it is well hidden,' said Michael. 'Come on, we'll start again.' But everywhere was soon reexamined. They were both at a loss. Michael rubbed his chin.

'The answer is probably simple if we could only see it,' he muttered, half to himself.

'Could it be outside?' asked Ariadne. 'What is there behind this place?'

'Just garden, a huge patio and a path reaching down to the cliff edge where it meanders away forming steps and terraces down to the shore.'

'Nothing there then . . . The answer must lie here.' She turned away to look again, and caught sight of the fly-trap plant.

'Paulo said he kept the fly-trap plant on the altar to make sacrifice. I don't know if he was joking.'

Michael came to stand in front of it. 'The only place we haven't searched well. Here give me a hand to move it.'

'There's no need. Look there . . . ' Ariadne pointed to a leaf, tightly jammed into a crevice of the front stone of the altar! They looked at one another.

Michael ran a questing finger along

the crack. He knelt to see better. But there was no knob or any other joint. He sat back on his heels, and surveyed the whole length, and in front. Then he gave a smothered exclamation.

'There it is. See the join where the front steps join the side pieces.' The uprights of the steps were all carved, with flowers and grapes and vine-leaves, and in the middle and at the two ends there were fiendish faces of satyrs staring out with blind eyes. Michael examined one of them, and pressed both eyes. The left one appeared to move a little, the groove round the eye appearing less dusty than the other. He pressed again, harder, and was rewarded by a creaking. Holding his finger on the bulbous eye, he watched the top step turn back on itself, and further stone steps were revealed below.

When the movable stonework came to rest, it resembled the baluster of a stone staircase, and at the bottom of the six steps was a door. It opened easily, and the air coming up from the low continuing passageway was stale but not foetid.

'This is it, Ariadne. This tunnel runs under the stone pathway outside. I'll take you back to the house now and get my torch. I'm going after Paulo.'

'I'll come too. I could be of help.'

'No. I want you to stay with Anyah. She too is suffering. Now I must go alone. It is between him and I. Besides, there will be Takis, and Stephanos and Petros. We four can bring him back!'

'But Michael . . .'

'Please, darling . . . I should feel better if I knew you were safe.'

'Very well, Michael, but please hurry. Anyah and I will not rest until we see you again.'

They fought their way back to the house. Anyah was relieved to see them, and surprised at the news of the entry to an underground tunnel.

'My father always insisted there was a tunnel running under the sea to the island. He said thousands of years ago, all the Greek islands were part of the mainland and after a series of earthquakes some of the land was swamped. That tunnel could be so old that it was there before the Myceneans invaded Greece . . . '

'It must have been a private passageway for the priests. Anyhow I am going to explore it and look for Paulo. Ariadne is staying with you, Anyah.'

'Then you must eat before you go. There is coffee on the hob, and the remains of the moussaka . . . '

'There's no time for food. I must be off . . . '

'Michael Gavalas, you don't leave this house before you eat! The very idea! And you too, Miss. You look as if you need something inside you. Come on now, into the kitchen. It won't take long.'

She glared at Michael, who glared back and then he smiled.

'Good old Anyah! You never change. I remember you stopping Paulo and I rushing off on some escapade in the same way. All right, I'll eat. I could do with something anyway, and I wouldn't like to get into your bad books!' He grinned and gave her a quick hug.

Anyah was right. They both felt better after they had eaten. Then Ariadne watched him go, fearful of the outcome. She helped Anyah to shoot the bolts when he had gone, but not before he took her into his arms and whispered in her ear,

'Take heart, my love. I'll find Paulo and bring him back. I must hurry now, for there may be other lives at stake. Fortunately Takis and he have always been friendly . . . the others, he does not know. It would only take a little spark . . . ' She nodded; a sudden lump in her throat made speech difficult.

He kissed her and she clung to him.

'Be careful. I'll pray for you . . . Do you think the tunnel will be safe?'

'If Paulo has been using it regularly, then it must be safe! Now I must go.'

After the bolts were in place she followed Anyah to her own sitting-room. They were prepared for a night-long vigil. For a while she prowled the room like a cat, too restless to settle. Anyah watched her in silence. She had taken up one of Paulo's socks and was darning. She finished the hole neatly and then laid it with its mate. She got up and went to a chest of drawers. Riffling underneath several items she brought out a photograph album.

'Come, sit beside me, and I will show you my most treasured snaps.' She laid the book flat on a small table in front of them.

Ariadne's interest was caught. The book was filled with black and white pictures taken evidently by an amateur. Some were blurred and out of focus, others taken by a shaking hand. Anyah looked at them and laughed.

'The bad ones were taken by the boys. At one stage, they spent all their pocket money on films. Sometimes when Michael came to stay he would bring several films from Athens and they were trigger-happy for a few days. Look, that one is of Paulo when he was just a small boy before Michael was born.' He was in Anyah's arms and waving his arms. Anyah was dark and very much slimmer in those days. But from the way she held Paulo, to anyone who knew, could be seen the look of proud motherhood.

They were all of Paulo, his father and Anyah. So Mrs Gavalas must have been dead by then, reflected Ariadne. He seemed a normal merry little boy, very like his father. When had the change really started? Surely before the incident of the village girl?

Then there seemed to be a gap, and then Michael as a small boy appeared with Paulo. Michael on a donkey . . . Michael and Paulo on a cart with Anyah . . . both together fishing, a proud Michael holding up his first fish, and many more. Ariadne was interested to see that there were no pictures of Michael's father.

'Did Michael always come here alone? There are no pictures of Michael's parents here.'

'No, Angelica Dounas had no time for the island. She was town-bred and preferred Athens. She died when Michael was three. And his father never came again after they fought over me . . . He was badly wounded and nearly died. That was when he found out about Paulo.'

'You said there were two occasions they nearly killed each other.'

'Yes. They fought first time when they first met me. I came to the house with some laundry sent by my mother. We all laughed and joked, and I was flattered. I was only fifteen at the time, and they not much older. I was amazed at two boys being so alike . . . They both wanted me . . . and they quarrelled and then fought. Paulo's father carried a knife scar to his dying day.'

'How dreadful!'

'Not at all. I was proud that two

such good-looking well-bred young men should think enough about me to fight!'

'But weren't you frightened?'

'Not then. I was too young and silly. Years later I was appalled at the damage I had unwittingly done. I separated two brothers who until then, lived for each other.' The old woman sighed. 'And when I found out that Angelica Dounas had borne a child, not her husband's, I did all I could to help. The shock of it brought out a hidden instability that was in both twins. When Michael came here to stay for long periods it was because his father was in a mental home undergoing treatment. Michael Gavalas was right when he knew he shouldn't marry!'

'But why did you not tell him about his real father? It would have eased his agony. I can't forgive you for that!'

'I was wrong. He did not seem interested in women. I wanted him to remain here with Paulo. I was frightened for Paulo. I wanted someone to love him and be with him after I am gone . . . I thought those tendencies in Paulo would die away . . . He seemed happy and content with Michael, until you came back to Xanos.'

'But I knew nothing of all this! I am not to blame!'

'Forgive me, I did not mean you were to blame. Now, I know I was wrong and Michael should marry you and lead a normal life. But I never thought the husband of Nina Kavouras would ever return to Xanos, or bring a daughter, the living image of poor Paulo's Demeter! Until then, I think Paulo was resigned to losing her. Now, anything can happen!'

'We must go away from this place after this is all over. Michael and I must make a new life.'

'But will he go away and leave Paulo alone? Michael has a great deal of love for Paulo . . . and more than his share of loyalty. Can you see him leaving him to his fate?' They stared at one another, and it was as if deathly cold fingers had touched her heart . . . Ariadne turned her back on Anyah, biting her lips. She saw her dream of happiness dissolving into hazy mist.

9

Anyah suggested more coffee, and as they sat comfortably together for a while, Anyah told Ariadne about the young Michael. He had not been an angelic child, but mischievous and high-spirited. Sometimes he quarrelled with Paulo.

But there was an over-all picture of a little boy welcomed into a rather remote, lonely family. Paulo's father too, had shown his brother's son great kindness, even though he knew he was no Gavalas.

There had been no great proof of love between them, but he had done his duty and above all, fostered the love of the two boys for each other . . . Anyah herself, had loved Michael for himself, for the mischievous impulsive boy who had often flung his arms tight around Anyah and said,

'Anyah, I *do* love you so! Some day I am going to grow up and marry you!'

They were smiling together over some reminiscence, when there came a thunderous knocking on the outer door. They looked at each other, both with the same thought in mind. Was it Michael back again . . . or Paulo?

They hurried to the door and with some difficulty pulled back the bolts. When they finally did so it was to find an exhausted Professor and Elias Haralambos standing there, wet through and shivering. Ariadne smothered a gasp.

'Ariadne, thank God we've found you. We've looked all over the island for you.'

'Why, what ever has happened?' Ariadne felt a sudden fear.

'Don't keep the man talking there! Come into my kitchen, where it is warm,' said Anyah, taking charge. 'A bowl of hot soup, after a glass of wine is what you need right now.' She led the way to the kitchen. 'Now both of you sit beside the fire, and I'll find some dry clothes of the boys for you. Ariadne, pour them some wine. The bottle and glasses are over there.' She bustled away to find the clothes.

'Daddy, what is it? You've had a great shock. I can see it in your face.' She looked from him to Elias who was polishing his glasses, for they had steamed up in the warmth of the kitchen. 'Daddy, what *is* it? You're frightening me!' The Professor spoke with difficulty.

'We must evacuate the island! There has been a weather report from the Met Office to say that a hurricane is heading this way! And by its course, we could possibly be in the eye of it! We must get out within six hours.' He slumped, an exhausted pathetic figure. 'All my work wasted. Years of patient toil and research gone, finished . . .'

'But, Daddy, it will still be there afterwards! After all a hurricane is just a strong wind, isn't it?' She looked round to the others. 'What is the matter?'

'Darling, you've never experienced a hurricane. It can tear up everything in its path, and the wind brings rain, lots of it and the tide runs high. So high, all this island is in danger!'

Anyah, coming into the room with an armful of clothes gave a great cry.

'But what of Paulo and Michael! They are in the biggest danger of all. Out there on Demeter's Island they will stand no chance at all!' The Professor frowned and looked from one to another.

'What is this about Paulo and Michael?' Elias intervened.

'Alexander and Stephanos are out there too. They left in mid-afternoon to explore the island with the idea of landing a boat at high tide. They've not been back since.'

'It was madness! Why was I not told?' Elias shrugged.

'I thought you would know. It was not my business to inform you.

They are grown men . . . Besides, Takis Pappadopolous was with them. I consider him a safe man to be with.'

'They should have asked my advice. I could have warned them!'

'Takis knew the hazards, better than you. They all went into it with their eyes open.'

'But now, what shall we do?'

Anyah moved forward with two steaming bowls.

'First you eat, and then consider, and when you are ready, change into these woollens and waterproofs. You will need them!'

But while the Professor had been protesting, Ariadne had made up her mind.

'Daddy, I'm going after Michael . . . Tonight we found an opening into a tunnel that goes from here over to Demeter Island. And Michael went down it to look for Paulo. He fears the worst.'

'A priests' tunnel eh? I have often wondered about the possibility of another means of access. I should like to see it. I'll come with you, Ariadne.'

'No, no, Daddy. Your place is with Eugenie. I love Michael, and I want to be with him. If we are to die . . . ' and her voice faltered, 'I should like to see him again, and feel his arms around me. I must go alone.'

'Little fool! You are my daughter and my concern. Eugenie is on board a Naval cutter, standing by. All our effects and specimens are aboard and even now, evacuation plans are going into force. I am coming with you. Elias, you take Anyah back to Xanos and look after her. Is there anyone else here tonight?'

Anyah shook her head.

'The two gardeners live out, and our two girls had permission to go into Xanos tonight to a wedding party.'

'Good. Then they will be aboard one of the boats by now. Get your valuables, Anyah, and Elias, waste no time getting back to Xanos.' Elias blinked his eyes, behind his huge glasses. He looked like a frightened owl.

'I would rather you came too. Those steep bends in the road, and there could be other landslides . . . I'm not a good driver.' Anyah snorted.

'I know that road blindfold. I'll keep you right. If they want to warn Paulo and Michael, and help them, we have no right to stop them. The Lord have mercy on us all!' She crossed herself.

Ariadne noticed that the first thing she picked up to take with her was her photograph album . . . She then went off to her bedroom and a few minutes later came back with a bundle neatly tied.

'I'm ready,' she said calmly. She looked around the warm comfortable kitchen. 'This has been my home for a lifetime. So many memories . . . ' She sighed and raised her head. 'Well, Kírios Haralambos, are you ready?'

'Yes, yes, if you are sure . . . ?'

'Of course, man,' said the Professor irritably. 'For God's sake, act like a man and get Anyah to the boats before it is too late!'

'But what of you both? How will you get away?'

'It is all in the hands of the Gods . . . or God. If Takis is still on the island with the other men and his boat is intact we shall have as good a chance as any other small boat, especially if we get away before the full blast of the storm. Now go, and Elias, get a message to the Naval Commander to keep a watch on Demeter Island. We might need his help. Now good luck, and God be with you.'

Anyah laid two powerful torches down on the table.

'I found them in Paulo's room. You will need them.' She looked over at Ariadne and her mouth quivered. Then they were in each other's arms, crying.

'I'll pray for you all,' she muttered and then she and Elias let themselves out of the house.

The Professor took Ariadne in his arms. For a moment nothing was said, but both knew and felt the bond of love. Then he put her gently aside.

'I think I've been a rotten father, dear. I should never have brought you back to Xanos. I knew it was a mistake as soon as we landed. I sensed it was wrong . . . One can't bring back the dead. But I was too absorbed and selfish in my work. Can you forgive me?'

'Daddy, if you had never brought me back I should never have known Michael . . . I may never know perfect happiness . . . but I have had a glimpse. Some people never even experience that!'

They quickly collected what they thought might be necessary. Ariadne stuffed bread and cheese and a bottle of wine into her pockets and the Professor found Anyah's long nylon wash-line and wound it roughly around his waist, and picked up a sharp kitchen-knife . . .

Soon they were ready and with difficulty they slipped out of the door and closed it behind them. Ariadne showed her father where the knob was to reveal the steps. For a moment he forgot the imminent danger to examine the ingenuity of the mechanism.

'Come *on*, Daddy! We must get this door open and start on the journey. It could easily cave in you know, with the storm.' The Professor came back to the present with an effort. Ariadne showed her irritation and highly tense state by hammering on the door.

'Darling, that doesn't help. You will wear yourself out. Let me try.' His experience in these matters soon had the door open, and he shone the powerful torch down the stone stairs, and on into the blackness. 'Come on then, Ariadne, it looks safe enough at the moment. Let's get this door shut again.'

'But why? Wouldn't it be safer to leave it open? We might want to get out again quickly.'

'Not this way, darling. Remember Atlantis?' Ariadne nodded, too startled to speak. 'Well, the Met Office expects this island to finish up under the waves. Do you understand? So closing this door will stop the sea filling up the passage too quickly.'

'But what of Demeter Island?'

'Yes, it too is doomed!'

'Then what are we standing here for? Let's get there and warn the others.' Ariadne started running down the rough, worn steps. 'Wait. A headlong fall isn't going to help. Take it steady. I don't want you with a sprained ankle or broken leg.' Ariadne stopped her headlong descent and waited for her father to catch up.

'I'm sorry. I'm beginning to panic. I didn't know I was so claustrophobic. I want to get through this tunnel to the other side. I would rather drown with the sky above rather than be drowned like a rat in a sewer!'

'Come on then. Put your torch out and hold my hand. I'll lead and we'll make faster time. Try and forget everything but this one job of getting through. We'll worry about the rest later.'

But this was easier said than done. As they stumbled down the dry stone steps, the vision of Michael drowning or being harmed by Paulo came before her. And the greatest nightmare of all was that he should die before she got to him. Not to see the love in his eyes again would be agony, and not to hear his voice . . . or to tell him all the things she had been too shy to say.

The steps terminated in a long flat tunnel for a few yards and then there were perhaps another fifty steps. Ariadne realized they were moving down the terraces to the beach below the villa. At last the steps gave off to a damp tunnel with brackish water standing nearly ankle-deep. The rock walls dripped water, and Ariadne found to her cost that small stones had been washed into the passage. She tripped over one of them and if her father had not been clasping her hand she would have fallen.

Now the way was rougher, and in some parts the tunnel was so low that they were nearly bent double. There was a strange moaning lapping noise from far away and Ariadne realized, with fear, that it was the faint sound of the sea. They were now somewhere between the main island and the little island of Demeter! Her hand convulsively tightened on her father's.

'Careful now. Don't panic,' said her father. 'We're nearly over the other side. I've been counting my steps, and I can make a rough guess as to how far Demeter is. Are you all right?'

'My ankle hurts, and I've got a cut on my knee I think, but it's not bothering me.'

'Good girl. You are doing very well. It could be not much farther. I feel the floor of the tunnel rising slightly.'

'Daddy, do you think we'll get onto the island easily. There could be another door.'

'If Michael managed, we can. Where

they can go, we can. Keep that in your head.'

'I'm getting more frightened, Daddy. I fear the worst . . .'

'Hush now. Do you want me to slap your face?' His voice was like a whiplash. 'I want no hysterical woman here!'

'I'm sorry, Daddy. I'll try to be calm.'

There was an old door, once stout and strong, with rusted primitive hinges. Now it swung loose, a greyish-black mass eaten by time. The torch light showed slimy green walls with beads of sweat trickling down them. Snails and fat white slugs glowed in the light. A furtive movement showed there was life down there in the Stygian darkness. Ariadne shuddered and clung convulsively to her father, biting her lip until she tasted blood.

'Steady, girl. You're doing fine. We're nearly out of it. See, the ground is rising. Soon we'll be out of this stinking water.' Ariadne did not answer. If she had opened her mouth she would have screamed.

Then came the steps again, and she gave a prayer of thankfulness. Anything to face on Demeter itself would be easy if she could see the blessed sky!

The steps were well-worn where many feet had rested. At some time in the dim past the tunnel must have been a busy thoroughfare, probably before the great deluge. A private means of reaching Demeter's temple in days when marauders and enemies abounded.

But now it was a decaying smelly place in danger of being engulfed by the sea, and Ariadne was relieved when they reached a higher level and the tunnel ran smooth and dry.

The tunnel ended in a small dank room that smelled badly of fungus. Again, there were stone stairs leading upwards. But this time the stairs led to a long corridor with several openings. They paused to take their bearings.

Ariadne stood shivering and teeth

chattering while her father explored the openings. The cold was the penetrating cold of the grave.

'Now stand still and don't move from here, darling, while I take a look over there. Keep your torch out, but when I return, I'll turn my torch on and off so you will know it is me. You signal in return and then I will know exactly where you are. Right?'

'Very well, but don't be long. I'm chilled to the bone.'

'Get your bottle of wine out and have a drink, and jump up and down and swing your arms. I'll not be long.'

She watched the light grow smaller and then disappear. He must have turned a corner! The darkness seemed to grow blacker and suffocating. Now she really knew what it was like to be truly claustrophobic. She slipped her torch on for a moment while she fumbled with the wine. It was only lightly corked having been opened previously by Anyah. It trickled down her throat in a warm wave. The rough red wine did the trick, it was warming and gave her added confidence. She watched impatiently for her father and when at last he returned she gave the signal in anticipation of an early move.

'Not much luck that way. One opening leads to a burial chamber. I wish I had plenty of time to examine it . . . The other, also interesting, is some kind of Priest's chamber . . . We must go this way.' She followed closely behind him, but now she felt better, and blessed the grape.

Another opening revealed a store room. There were the remains of pottery oil-pitchers and tall graceful jars containing dust. The Professor tipped one up, and commented,

'Hm, herbs, I should think. The priests used quantities of herbs for burning and strewing on the floors. I really should take some of this dust for analysis . . . '

'Daddy, for goodness sake come along! Why think of that when none of us might be here tomorrow!'

'Sorry, darling. I get carried away. Come on, this is the last opening. It *must* lead upwards.'

It did indeed. But not before they passed several cubicles, which must have served the priests as sleeping quarters, as each stone cell-like room had a raised stone slab, evidently to lie on.

But now the air was fresher, and the stone steps gave way to marble. They came to a huge doorway decorated with carvings. The topmost carving was of a woman with all kinds of animals at her feet. The Professor played his light over her. Ariadne saw the face of a beautiful kindly woman who smiled down with love at a fawn looking up at her. She was struck by the look of complete motherhood.

'Well, this is it, darling. The doorway to the temple of Demeter, mother of the Earth and Goddess of Fertility. Shall we go in?'

'Daddy, what do you think we shall

find? What about Paulo and Michael?'

'Darling, we must go in to find out . . .'

'What is that noise? That peculiar humming and moaning sound. I have just become aware of it.'

'I don't know. I've just become aware of it myself. Come on, let's open this door and find out!'

The creaking door opened easily. It was as if it had been newly oiled. But the minute they stepped through, the noise increased a thousand-fold.

'What can it be?' shouted Ariadne into her father's ear.

'The wind. It must be the wind! Remember the hurricane? It will be all hell let loose outside,' he shouted back. 'Turn your torch on so we can see where we are.' Both beams circled the huge cavern. It was a temple hewn out of the living rock!

It was more like a series of arched recesses. Great pillars of rock as it had been, all those years ago held up a massive arched roof. It was so high

212

that the combined light from the two torches failed to penetrate the darkness. But along the walls at the height of a man were blackened holders that once had contained blazing torches.

They moved around the chamber and found each recess had its own plinth for a statue. Excitedly, the Professor pointed out part of a crumbling statue.

'I do believe that is a statue of Persephone, Demeter's daughter, who was supposed to be held for part of the year by Pluto, king of the underworld! Each time he allowed her to re-visit her mother it was Spring, and there was a stirring of all things growing underground. And the Greeks held their festivals in honour of Spring and the Great Earth Mother. A wonderful legend.'

'I can do without the legends, Daddy. All I want to do is get out of here!'

'Gently, gently. We must go carefully. Take your torch and look for an opening. Go that way and I'll go this way.'

They parted and for a while Ariadne could see the narrow beam of light. Then it vanished behind a pillar and she was alone.

She stumbled along slowly, hating every moment of the search. Once she trod on something soft and she smothered a scream and tried to run, not wanting to turn her torch on the object. She didn't want to know . . .

Then she found what they were both looking for. A flight of crumbling steps. She played her torch upwards. Yes, this must be it! The thought of re-tracing her footsteps to find her father was daunting, but it would have to be done.

She decided to give a shout first. After all he would not be far away, perhaps in one of the recesses. But he should have been walking down the opposite side of the cavern. She was suddenly uneasy. Her cry when it came out of her numbed throat was low and frightened.

'Daddy! Daddy, are you there?' She listened with ears straining. Nothing but the plop of unseen water. She moistened her lips to try again. There was a feeling of movement rather than sound and a hand was clapped over her mouth and Michael's angry voice whispered,

'Ariadne! What in hell's name are you doing here?'

10

Ariadne felt Michael's arms close round her, and she sagged with relief. For one horrible moment she had thought the hand was Paulo's, and had tried to scream. Michael shook her gently.

'I thought I told you to stay safe with Anyah. This place is not fit for you to wander about in, besides you are wet. You had no business coming here!'

'Oh Michael, Michael, stop wittering on and kiss me. Daddy's here too. I'll tell you about it in a minute, but now, just hold me and kiss me, and Michael, tell me you love me, before it is too late.'

'Too late for what, sweet?'

'Just kiss me. I'll explain in a minute.'

The kiss was satisfying to both, and Michael murmured endearing nothings into her ear, and Ariadne responded so ardently it shocked her sense of propriety. If she had doubts of their love they were now dispersed . . . Shaken with emotion, she sighed and pushed him away.

'Now tell me why you are here. Paulo has Takis and the other men holed up. He's armed, Ariadne. He'd gone back to the villa to get his father's Resistance revolver, and he's in such a mood he'll use it at a flicker of an eyelash . . . and keep your voice down. He's up above there in Apollo's own temple. If he sees you he will go berserk!'

'Daddy and I came to warn you about the hurricane. Have you been outside? We saw from the villa that the tide was higher in the harbour than it's ever been. What time is it? Have you any idea? Daddy said we had six hours before we were in the centre of the storm. He is back there somewhere, looking for a way out.'

'Then we must go and find him. There are dozens of tunnels and openings over there. One passage was used by the common people to come over to the holy island to intercede for help and to bring gifts for the Goddess. The people of Xanos fed the Priests and their Priestesses in that way. Come on, we'll back-track. He can't be very far away.'

But there was no sign of him and Michael cursed under his breath.

'Now what am I going to do with you while I go looking for him?'

'I'm coming with you. I'm not staying alone.'

'But I'm going to the upper level. Paulo is up there somewhere. I came down here to try and find another way into the great Sun temple. Paulo does not know I am here yet. I want to take him by surprise.'

'But have we got time? Daddy thinks this whole island and Xanos itself will be drowned. Don't you understand? I *must* come with you.'

Michael turned the torch onto his watch.

'It is nearly midnight. Come on, let's find your father while we calculate how much time we have.' He took her hand and quietly they moved away across the cavern floor.

Ariadne soon found out the reason for her father's disappearance. The cavern wall at this side was intersected with passages. It could be difficult finding him. They ventured up two of them and then Michael had the notion to examine the ground. In these passages the floor was covered in fine sand.

'No one's been this way for a long time. Look, the sand is undisturbed. We must try another path.'

At last they found signs of a scuffle. The opening was bigger than the rest and when Michael played his torch on to the tunnel walls he found distinct traces of carvings.

'Hm, I think we have stumbled on another way up to the Sun temple. Probably the High Priest's apartments. But by the imprints on the ground, I think Paulo has intercepted your father! He must have forced him up to the top level.'

'Oh Daddy, Daddy, why did I leave you? Oh, what can we do? Will he kill him?'

'No. I don't think so. I think your father is just a nuisance to him. Alexander and Stephanos are in most danger. They are the ones who threaten his temple. They were looking for that Nazi gold, remember? I wonder if they ever got the chance to find it?'

'What are we going to do?'

'He mustn't find you, or he would take it as a sign that Demeter had come home . . . Oh, I don't underestimate Paulo. I think he has gone over the edge . . . All I want to do is find him and take him somewhere safe where he may get treatment.'

'But will we get off this island? What about the sea?'

'Darling, I scouted round earlier on. There is a jagged pinnacle of rock which rears up far above the rest.

We must make for that and sit out the storm.'

'What about Takis's boat? Couldn't we risk that?'

'What, in *that* sea? It would be madness, and I don't suppose it will have survived. Always providing it was intact when they landed.'

'You don't think . . . ?'

'I don't think anything,' he said irritably. 'It's taken me all my time to find my way around here. I'm not familiar with it as Paulo is.'

Michael carefully felt his way up the broad stone steps. They were more ornate than the others they had climbed. These had the shine of marble even though yellowed and green with damp and discolouration. Near the top he doused his light. No need to advertise the fact they were there.

They paused to listen, but Ariadne could only hear the sound of her heartbeats. They seemed so loud she wondered if Paulo could hear them.

Now there was more light, and dimly from way up high, they could just discern a glimpse of navy-blue sky and the odd twinkling star, before scudding clouds obliterated the view.

'Look up there,' whispered Michael into her ear, his voice just a breath of sound. 'Can you hear me? That is the great Sun window above the altar of Apollo. There will be a statue underneath. Paulo will probably be near it somewhere.'

She nodded, and then nearly screamed. Something had brushed her cheek in the darkness. Michael clapped his hand over her mouth.

'Bats,' he muttered. 'Keep still.' She turned in his arms, buried her head tightly into his chest and shuddered.

But the rustle of bats' wings had done what they had not done. They had alerted Paulo. There was the sound of movement down below the great window.

'Anyone there? If that is Michael, come down to the altar. I have

Professor Powis here . . . tied up and safe.' Ariadne gave a smothered gasp and wanted to run towards the altar. Michael held her back.

'Fool!' he hissed. 'You're playing into his hands! Keep back, I don't think your father's told him you are down here.'

'But Daddy!'

'All right for the moment I think. Keep quiet!' They stood mute and waited.

The silence seemed to stretch into hours. They heard Paulo's feet scraping the rocks. Suddenly he lost patience.

'Don't play games with me, boy! I know you are there! Come out and show yourself. Look, I'm lighting a torch so you can come down to the altar . . .'

A moment elapsed and then Ariadne saw a huge torch made of wood dipped in oil flare up. Black smoke from it poured upwards to the great window where it was sucked away. Paulo suddenly screamed.

'Damn you, Michael! This is no time for hide-and-seek! Come out and face me like a man . . . or are you frightened?' He laughed a low menacing laugh, and Ariadne felt Michael stiffen. 'You can hear me? I *know* you are there. The bats don't fly around in panic for nothing. I have your friends, you will be pleased to know. Rounded them up before they could even get their bearings. Fools! But I must admire their ingenuity for landing on the island during the meltemi, as did other sailors long years ago. And I admire my old friend Pappadopolous's skill in sailing so close to the rocks. Alas, the boat has gone. We're marooned here until the storm dies down . . . Are you listening, Michael? I am standing by a lever here, that will flood the whole of the lower levels. A precaution of the Priests in case of invasion by their enemies. Come into the open, Michael or I shall pull this lever . . . I mean it, man, and I don't want to harm you. I give you my word . . . '

224

'Can we trust him?' whispered Ariadne.

'I'm going to gamble on it. I'm going down to reason with him, and try and persuade him to leave the island quietly.'

'Shall I come too. Perhaps if he knows I am here, you could be wrong, he might want us all to get away.'

'No. He must not see you. I think you would be the spark . . . '

'Michael, I am waiting . . . ' Paulo's voice had taken on a sing-song note.

'Run back, Ariadne, and hide in one of the alcoves. Try and find some rock to hide behind. He'll not wait much longer. Keep your chin up.' He gave her a quick hug and a kiss. 'Wish me luck!'

She watched him move stealthily forward in the dim light given by the torch. When he was in the main aisle of the temple he showed himself boldly. He moved down towards the altar to a pleased chuckle from Paulo. He stepped into the light of the torch and

Ariadne saw the glint of the revolver in his hand . . .

It was then, she disappeared into the shadows of the alcoves, and stumbled in the darkness trying to feel her way to a hiding-place. She dreaded stirring up the bats again. They would be a dead give-away and Paulo was astute enough to know who would be there . . . She heard Michael's voice, faint, but carrying as she crept away,

'Paulo, we must talk somewhere. Put down the gun, Paulo . . . ' and then the voice became a murmur and then silence . . .

Ariadne kept walking and stopping to listen, but all around her was silence. The tunnel she found herself in apparently ran parallel with the great hall. Alcoves or small rooms seemed to cut into it. Probably priests' domestic quarters, but by her reckoning she was walking towards the altar end of the hall. She still had not found a place to hide. These cell-like places had no cover, she must move on.

Then as she pressed against the wall, now fearful of discovery, she fell backwards. A huge stone had turned on a pivot. She had fallen through and the stone had returned to its position. She picked herself up and risked playing her torch over the walls. She found stairs ahead, dry, and evidently not used. She could hide there in the passage!

For a while she stayed there, and then her breath and courage returned and curiosity made her climb the stairs. They came out onto a little balcony overlooking the altar. A lookout for the priests, no doubt. Far down below she could see Paulo, but where was Michael? As she watched Paulo strode into the light of the flaming torch. He was dressed in white flowing robes and there was something on his yellow curly hair, and in his right hand the blue-glint of a revolver . . .

And then as she watched she saw with horror that the light was fast approaching. The first sun's rays of early morning were bursting through the great Sun Window, down, down, down to where she was standing. And as she watched, Paulo turned to greet the sun with up-stretched arms to pray . . . and saw her!

He gave a great shout. She gasped and turned to run. But where? She looked down the stairs but knew he could well be on his way up. She looked upwards, and decided she had no choice. She pounded her way upwards, heart hammering in fear. The stairs ended in another balcony and a room just below the great window. The old door in front of her was ajar. She ran in and shut it, leaning back to regain her breath.

Now she realized she was at the top of the temple. The noise was indescribable. The wind came in gusts through the open slit windows, and sounded like the moaning of all the souls in hell. There was more rain in the wind. The old stones creaked until Ariadne felt sure the lookout tower would blow away.

For that was where she was. She could see far out to sea, this place built specially for the temple guards to watch from and wait for approaching enemies.

The view outside the window made her gasp with horror. The boiling sea had crept up the rocks. Where once Demeter Island had been inaccessible owing to sheer cliffs, now the waves dashed themselves against the upper ramparts. Craning her head to catch a glimpse of Xanos she was sure the harbour had disappeared. The mighty rollers were travelling at dizzying speed towards the lower crumbling white houses on Xanos. As she watched, she saw the boiling mass hit the houses and recede leaving devastation behind.

Then the struggling sun's rays disappeared behind sullen black clouds. And again the world turned dark.

The lookout room was round, with nothing in it but the droppings of birds and the remains of nests and egg-shells. She crouched by the window, like a rabbit trapped by a fox, her eyes fixed on the doorway.

She heard the furtive footsteps before the door slowly opened. She held her breath and as Paulo stepped inside, she expelled it audibly.

'So! You came at last! But why turn shy and run away? I've come to take you down to your quarters. Come, Demeter, and be my salvation!' He walked towards her holding out his hand. She pressed herself into the wall.

'Keep away from me! I came to look for Michael. I'm not your Demeter . . .' He laughed.

'Foolish child! Of course you do not remember! You need me to fulfil your destiny. You have been re-incarnated and you do not realize it. I must teach you the truths again. You and I can reign supreme. We can change the ways of men and start the golden age . . . Demeter, I have waited so long. Do not disappoint me again!'

'But I'm not Demeter!' She tried to run past him to the door, but his arm shot out and he pulled her to him. His teeth drew back, reminding Ariadne of a wolf . . .

'You're mine! Whether willingly or not . . . You and I shall have a son and then I shall be perfect in the eyes of Zeus. Only *then* will I gain Heavenly Immortality. I am tired of trying and failing. *This* time nothing shall go wrong. The Goddess of Fertility and the Great Apollo producing the perfect child!' He bent his head to kiss her, and she struggled to free herself.

Suddenly there was a crash of thunder overhead. Paulo recoiled and his hand slackened, but Ariadne was too frightened to run. It sounded like the end of the world.

Outside, the forked lightning ran merrily up and down the sky followed by a quick series of thunderous crashes. It was like a bombardment.

Paulo fell on his knees to pray.

'Oh my Father, I asked you for a sign. You sent Demeter back to me, so was that not good? But why the thunder and lightning? Do I displease you in some way? In my heart I know I have always done as you asked . . . ever since the day you revealed to me that I was Apollo, so many years ago. I have waited and suffered without complaint. Surely now my punishment for causing Demeter's untimely death is nearly over? Take away the guilt and give me peace!'

Ariadne listened in awe, fear giving way to pity. This man was in a hell of his own! He went on,

'Demeter reincarnated again, is surely that sign? You would not extend that punishment again and again into the future? To come together, only to part? If so, I would that I were dead and resting for a while to gather up my strength! Oh Zeus, Oh Father, I commend to you my body and my spirit!' He rose from his knees and gazed at Ariadne blindly. He was muttering to himself.

'The fault is mine. I am not ready to father a son and Zeus the All-seeing knows this. Therefore I must wait for another life. The time is not yet right. I can see it now. This was the testing time . . . ' He stretched out his hand to Ariadne.

'Come, do not be afraid. I shall not hurt you. It was never my intention to do so. I thought the time was right for our coming together, but I was wrong. I shall take you to Michael. He will look after you.'

'And you? What will you do?'

'I am going to rest.' He gave her a smile of great sweetness with no hint of his dark side. It was as if he had suppressed the evil part of him. There came another streak of lightning and the noise of a thunder-bolt striking. Ariadne screamed. And in a moment came the thunder, ear-shattering, heart-stopping. And then came the first earth tremor. The walls of the temple lookout shook and a great crack appeared like magic.

'Quickly now, this way . . . Zeus speaks and he is not patient.' Ariadne followed Paulo out into the passageway and back down the stone steps. But now masonry was being dislodged, and the stairway was dangerous with loose stones.

Twice she stumbled and Paulo caught her, or she would have hurtled to the bottom. The sound of the wind had changed too. There was rain, and it came down as if all the clouds had burst together. It even seeped through the new cracks in the walls and trickled at first slowly down the stairs, and then faster and faster.

Paulo pulled her into another doorway, a direct passage leading to the altar. They came out into the main temple chamber just as another tremor, lasting a little longer than the first, began. Gasping in air that was now dust-laden, Ariadne fought her way to where the oil-soaked torch was still burning. Paulo was before her and bending over something with a knife in his hand.

For one horrible moment, Ariadne thought he was going to kill Michael, but Michael sat up. Paulo had cut the cords that bound him. He staggered to his feet and Ariadne ran to him like a homing pigeon. For one glorious moment they clung together.

'Thanks, Paulo.' They clasped hands and Paulo looked sorrowfully at Michael.

'This is good-bye, Michael . . . Remember me as I was when we were boys. I am what I am, nothing can change that. Look after Demeter for me. Some day we shall meet again.'

'Paulo, how do we get out? And where are Takis and Stephanos and Alexander and the Professor?'

'They are imprisoned in one of the rooms on the lower level. They desecrated Apollo's altar. They were looking at Apollo's gold when I found them. They were easy to take prisoner, especially when I waved the gun.' He grinned reminiscently. 'I've never seen men look so frightened! And as for the

Professor — he's close by.'

'Take us to them, Paulo. We must get to the surface. Then we may stand a chance. We could climb that high peak.'

Paulo took the burning torch and showed them where the Professor was laid tied up and then led the way down to the priests' quarters. One room had been sealed off by several boulders piled up in front of it. Paulo and Michael worked like madmen to shift enough to allow a man to move past. Another tremor came like the growl of a wild beast in the bowels of the earth. There was a great cracking sound as if the earth was splitting.

Ariadne, an arm about her father, waited in fear while Michael and Paulo went inside and freed the three frightened men. They emerged from the room rubbing numbed wrists and shivering.

'What do we do now?' Alexander's voice was a hoarse whisper.

'This way.' Paulo took charge and

they all followed. At one point they passed the opening to the underground passage to the main island. Michael who still had his torch, played the light down into the depths. Water was lapping at the bottom steps!

'No escape that way. The lower levels and the tunnel are swamped, and the water's rising. Look, it's up another step already!'

Ariadne gasped. She had a mad feeling of wanting to run and run and run. As if the world was undergoing the Flood all over again.

But Paulo knew where he was making for. There was a narrow stairway leading from the High Priest's chamber directly to the surface.

'Go straight up there, and you will come out directly onto a crop of rocks facing Xanos. It was there the High Priest came to bless the main island on Feast Days. From there, it is an easy matter to climb Apollo's Finger, the name for the tallest peak. There are footholds cut into the rock. I have sat there and watched Xanos many times and never been detected. You will be safe, as other rocks give shelter.'

'Thank you, Paulo. Why not come with us? We can all be saved. Paulo, I beg you!'

'Michael, I don't want to be saved. It is time I gave up this life and prepared for another. Next time, things will be different, I promise you . . . Good-bye, Demeter, we shall meet again never fear, and if we are lucky and Zeus wills, there will be a son.'

Takis moved impatiently, and then whispered,

'Begging pardon for interrupting, but if he's not coming, I think it is time we moved. Talking here isn't going to save us!'

Michael nodded.

'Everybody start climbing those stairs, and you, Ariadne, go between Takis and Stephanos. I'll follow in just a moment. I have something to say to Paulo.'

They started to climb. Ariadne, looking back, saw the cousins' hands clasp together . . . and then she was outside facing the fury of the wind and rain.

Afterwards she never really remembered how they managed to claw their way up that great spur of rock. But by pulling and pushing each other they managed it. At the top, they found enough shelter to keep them from blowing away, but they were soaked and squelching in their shoes.

Michael inched his way to her, and she lay in the comparative comfort of his arm. If she was to die, she could not think of a better place to be.

Takis struggled to his knees and clung to the escarpment as he tried to look across to Xanos. What he saw made him shout and sink back again. With a stunned face he turned to Michael and shouted in his ear.

'The island! It is gone. Nothing but sea and the tip of the mountains left.' Michael struggled to his feet. It was true. There were no houses, no church spire or white marble ruins of the old temple, just a jagged mass of rocks. Xanos had plunged again to the seabed.

Then he turned to their small island. The sea was much higher now and Michael could see that soon the upper temple would be flooded. Then he saw Paulo standing in the lookout, his ragged, tattered gown whipping his body. His hands were outstretched, and as he watched more stones fell and he was exposed to the full fury of the elements.

Ariadne stood up and clung to Michael and watched with him. She saw Paulo raise his arms into the air and look up into the sky. He seemed to smile, and then leapt out into space.

It all happened so quickly, that she could hardly credit that it had happened. But the rag-doll figure was caught by the wind and dashed down onto the rocks below. When she opened her eyes, the rag-doll was gone, sucked away into the sea ... She clung to Michael and they sank down together. His face was white and a tear coursed its way down his cheek.

11

To Ariadne it seemed hours and hours that they remained there. She brought out the bundle of bread and cheese, and they shared it and the rest of the wine that remained in the bottle. She found a capacious scarf in another deep pocket which she wrapped about her head, tucking her long hair underneath.

Takis was too upset to eat but sat shaking his head in utter disbelief in the desolation he had seen. His house, his garden and little vineyard all gone in a matter of hours. His boat too had gone, dashed to matchwood on the great rocks of Demeter Island. Now Takis was facing the fact he would have to make a new life for himself and his family on the mainland. He crossed himself. Always providing they got away from this accursed place and if his family were safe.

Then all of a sudden they realized there was a great silence, each one noticing it at the same time. But it was the silence of desolation. No birds wheeled and screamed. They stood up and faced Xanos. But for the few rocks standing up like jagged teeth, the sea covered everywhere.

'Perhaps the tide will uncover the island when it goes down,' muttered Alexander. Takis shook his head.

'The island is finished, and so is this one. Look! Half this island has disappeared. Only the upper heights remain. The temple has gone forever. Paulo Gavalas knew what would happen. This whole island was honeycombed with tunnels. We are lucky to be alive so far.'

'Do you still think there is danger?' said Michael.

'I think it is only a matter of time before all the underground workings crumble and disintegrate.'

'I agree with you,' said Stephanos. 'A pity we could not bring out that

German gold. It was there for the taking.'

'You found it then?' said Michael.

'Yes. And we were so excited about it that Paulo crept up on us unawares. It was hidden underneath the altar. A great pity. At least we know it's there and need look no farther.'

'And now lost for all time,' said Alexander. 'But I *did* bring up a handful of one ounce bars! Six to be precise. I was holding them when Paulo appeared. He waved us away from the box and told me to put down the lid. I did so and slid the bars into my pocket.' He pulled them out of his pocket to prove his words. They showed dull and dark in the light. 'Enough to prove to the authorities that we found the hoard. The last of the Nazi gold!' He carefully put them away again and zipped his pocket up. 'If we get out of this alive, Stephanos and I will need all the proof we can get to get paid for our efforts!' Alexander's bristly face split into a grin. 'They can't argue about them. They all bear the German hallmark. It was the first thing I looked for!'

They arranged to take turns in watching for passing craft. Now that the wind had dropped and the rain had ceased to lash down, there was hope of rescue. Michael took the first turn and the other men rested as best as they could. Ariadne chose to sit with Michael and talk while he watched.

Holding hands, they spoke of the future, and Ariadne gently told him about his mother.

'And so you see, Michael, you are not a Gavalas. Do you mind very much?'

Michael sat very quiet for a few minutes. His face was averted so Ariadne could not read his expression. Then he sighed. She took his hand in hers, and he patted it.

'Only for my father's sake. He was a very proud man. It must have hurt him very much because he loved my mother . . . I'm sure of that, despite his quarrel with my uncle over Anyah. I feel a great sense of relief, knowing I am not tainted . . . The thought has always haunted me, more so since meeting you. But I feel a little bereft. I always felt that whatever happened to me, I came from a good family. I was proud of the name and of my long ancestry. Now . . . I have no right to my name but I am strangely free!' He took her face between his hands and gently kissed her. 'It means our children too, will be free. Free of the insidious worry of wondering when the axe might fall! I suddenly feel a weight has been lifted from my shoulders!' He laughed happily and slipped an arm about her.

Suddenly, Professor Powis, who had been sitting quietly a little away from the others, rose to his feet. Apart from giving Ariadne a quick kiss and a hug when they were re-united, he had spoken little. He had been brooding on the loss of the ancient temple and what it all meant, in the nature of hard work.

He stretched his arms above his head and said,

'I'll take the next watch. This inactivity is driving me crazy.' Ariadne looked at him worriedly.

'Are you all right, Daddy?'

'As all right as I'll ever be. Why do you ask?'

'I don't know. You look . . . as if you have lost your way.'

'I have. My work swept away in a few hours. A way of life that has withstood thousands of years, relics just waiting to be found. All gone, finished, just memories. And that's how my own life's been. I've been sitting here, taking stock of myself. And what do I find?'

'Daddy, are you ill? I've never heard you in such a state before!'

'There you are! That bears out what I'm saying. I lost my wife because I was indifferent to her needs. I might have lost my daughter too. And I think I have lost her, oh, in the nicest possible way. You two are going to be married, I presume?'

Michael nodded.

'As soon as possible, sir. You have no objections?'

'None, my boy. I only wish I had my time over again, to enjoy her company before you found her. I regret deeply, my lack of friendship . . . not love, dear. I always loved you, even if I was too engrossed to show it. But last night's events have been a lesson to me. Nothing is permanent. We must live for the day. I am determined to re-shape my life. For me, values are going to change. People are going to be more important to me than anything else in the world.'

'Eugenie will help you, Daddy. She understands you and needs you too!'

'You don't mind?'

'Darling, I can marry Michael with an easy mind if I know you have Eugenie. We understand one another. She'll make you a wonderful wife!'

'Good, then that's settled. What are we waiting for?'

'But — but we've got to get off here

first!' she said laughing.

'That Naval cutter is sending a boat over. I've been watching it come in closer ever since I stood up.' He grinned like a boy. 'That surprises you, doesn't it?'

They both spun round to look out to sea, and Michael gave a great bellow and a wave. The other three jumped up, all nearly half-asleep. Then everyone was laughing and waving, and a small figure in the prow of the ship waved back.

'Daddy,' said Ariadne mischievously. 'I think your future is waving before you. Please wave back or she might change her mind.'

'Bless me, it *is* Eugenie! How in the world did she manage to persuade them to let her come looking for me!'

'You've always said Eugenie is efficient. From now on your life will be one long efficient dream!'

'I'm not sure if I'll like that, but I'm very willing to find out!'

Much later, when the business of

being transferred from island to boat and from boat to ship was satisfactorily negotiated, and they had all been fed and given dry clothes, Michael found a quiet corner on deck for himself and Ariadne. A tip in the right quarter and a broad-shouldered sailor stopped all and sundry from visiting that part of the deck.

'Comfortable? Want another cushion?'

'Yes. No. I can lay my head on your chest. I don't need another cushion.'

'Happy?'

'Huh-huh.'

'What does that mean?'

'What do you think?'

'Tell me then.'

'Don't you know?'

'Of course. But I want you to say it.'

'All right. I'm happy . . . because I'm with you.'

'You are going to marry me? Your father jumped the gun, but I want you to have a free choice, as long as it's yes.'

'Darling, of course it is yes. I wouldn't let you get away!'

Her arms slid around him, and he held her close and for a few moments there were only the soft murmurs of ecstasy and frustration. Then he raised his head but still held her close.

'Darling, will you mind just being a doctor's wife? There's no plantation any more, just a small vineyard in Greece and it doesn't pay very well. I've got a house . . . with a nice garden. It was my father's. But it is nothing compared to the Villa Spyros.'

'It will be our home. Anywhere we are together will be home to me. Do you not understand? I love you!'

'I'll never be anything but plain Doctor Gavalas, and you will have disturbed nights, probably by patients who can't pay, or don't do as I tell them. And I can be bad-tempered and boorish. Does the thought frighten you?'

'Not in the least! Do you *really* love me?'

'Of course. You must know that. I love you with every breath I take. How soon can we be married? I need you and I cannot wait much longer!'

Her answer was smothered by his kiss, but her heart answered for her.

'Soon, very soon, for I too cannot wait any longer!'

THE END

SAVAGE PARADISE
Sheila Belshaw

For four years, Diana Hamilton had dreamed of returning to Luangwa Valley in Zambia. Now she was back — and, after a close encounter with a rhino — was receiving a lecture from a tall, khaki-clad man on the dangers of going into the bush alone!

PAST BETRAYALS
Giulia Gray

As soon as Jon realized that Julia had fallen in love with him, he broke off their relationship and returned to work in the Middle East. When Jon's best friend, Danny, proposed a marriage of friendship, Julia accepted. Then Jon returned and Julia discovered her love for him remained unchanged.

PRETTY MAIDS ALL IN A ROW
Rose Meadows

The six beautiful daughters of George III of England dreamt of handsome princes coming to claim them, but the King always found some excuse to reject proposals of marriage. This is the story of what befell the Princesses as they began to seek lovers at their father's court, leaving behind rumours of secret marriages and illegitimate children.

THE GOLDEN GIRL
Paula Lindsay

Sarah had everything — wealth, social background, great beauty and magnetic charm. Her heart was ruled by love and compassion for the less fortunate in life. Yet, when one man's happiness was at stake, she failed him — and herself.

A DREAM OF HER OWN
Barbara Best
A stranger gently kisses Sarah Danbury at her Betrothal Ball. Little does she realise that she is to meet this mysterious man again in very different circumstances.

HOSTAGE OF LOVE
Nara Lake
From the moment pretty Emma Tregear, the only child of a Van Diemen's Land magnate, met Philip Despard, she was desperately in love. Unfortunately, handsome Philip was a convict on parole.

THE ROAD TO BENDOUR
Joyce Eaglestone
Mary Mackenzie had lived a sheltered life on the family farm in Scotland. When she took a job in the city she was soon in a romantic maze from which only she could find the way out.

NEW BEGINNINGS
Ann Jennings

On the plane to his new job in a hospital in Turkey, Felix asked Harriet to put their engagement on hold, as Philippe Krir, the Director of Bodrum hospital, refused to hire 'attached' people. But, without an engagement ring, what possible excuse did Harriet have for holding Philippe at bay?

THE CAPTAIN'S LADY
Rachelle Edwards

1820: When Lianne Vernon becomes governess at Elswick Manor, she finds her young pupil is given to strange imaginings and that her employer, Captain Gideon Lang, is the most enigmatic man she has ever encountered. Soon Lianne begins to fear for her pupil's safety.

THE VAUGHAN PRIDE
Margaret Miles

As the new owner of Southwood Manor, Laura Vaughan discovers that she's even more poverty stricken than before. She also finds that her neighbour, the handsome Marius Kerr, is a little too close for comfort.

HONEY-POT
Mira Stables

Lovely, well-born, well-dowered, Russet Ingram drew all men to her. Yet here she was, a prisoner of the one man immune to her graces — accused of frivolously tampering with his young ward's romance!

DREAM OF LOVE
Helen McCabe

When there is a break-in at the art gallery she runs, Jade can't believe that Corin Bossinney is a trickster, or that she'd fallen for the oldest trick in the book . . .

FOR LOVE OF OLIVER
Diney Delancey

When Oliver Scott buys her family home, Carly retains the stable block from which she runs her riding school. But she soon discovers Oliver is not an easy neighbour to have. Then Carly is presented with a new challenge, one she must face for love of Oliver.

THE SECRET OF MONKS' HOUSE
Rachelle Edwards

Soon after her arrival at Monks' House, Lilith had been told that it was haunted by a monk, and she had laughed. Of greater interest was their neighbour, the mysterious Fabian Delamaye. Was he truly as debauched as rumour told, and what was the truth about his wife's death?